GRAVE CREEK CONSPIRACY

GRAVE CREEK CONSPIRACY

A novel by

Daniel Isaac Morris

VICOA.COM
Pennsylvania, USA

ISBN-10 0982825021
ISBN-13 9780982825020
Published by Vicoa.com

Be sure to read *Grave Creek Connections*,
the book that precedes this one.

Other Morris books are:

Swaypole, a tale of mystery, populated with little people, carnies, ex-spies and mafia dons. The tale of intrigue is set in the mythical town of Gibsonton, WV

Cheat River, at the head of the Cheat is a plot that is too horrible to contemplate.

didyahavadaddy, a humorous look at the other side of public school education.

Riverfront Dreams, a look at homeowners associations and a search for sunken treasure in Florida. (Soon to be released)

Grave Creek Connections, a murderous cult operates among the citizens of a small Pennsylvania town.

Grave Creek Conspiracy, Eden Whitloe tries to solve "The Beautiful Maidens Murders" while a secret cult tries to keep its secrets and the murders from being discovered.

Available on line or at your favorite book store.

Be sure to visit http://www.dimorris.com

For the Morris, Rogers, Lambert and Kincaid Families.

For Barbara, Danny, Kelley
Webster and the late Ben Bird

This book is a work of fiction, and any similarities to places or persons, living or dead, is coincidental. While I refer to certain historical facts, be aware that these may at times be fictionalized and intentionally inconsistent with true historical accounts.

This book is a work of fiction, and any similarities to places or persons, living or dead, is coincidental. While I refer to certain historical facts, be aware that these may at times be fictionalized and intentionally inconsistent with true historical accounts. The book, Who Really Wrote the Book of Mormon? authored by Wayne L. Cowdery, Donald R. Scales, and Howard

A. Davis gives an account of the controversy concerning the founding of Mormonism and the Church of Jesus Christ of Latter Day Saints. The controversy is well documented, and this work neither supports nor disputes the authors' findings, since any controversy of a religious nature is settled as matter of belief and faith. I have the deepest respect for the beliefs, and particularly the family values, of the Church of Jesus Christ of Latter Day Saints.

The unfortunate scandals that involved a few individuals and took place at the New Vrindavan community in West Virginia are matters of historical and court record. There is no intention here to assign blame or judgment. I respect the Hare Krishna beliefs and the International Society for Krishna Consciousness (ISKCON).

There is a lovely county in the southwestern corner of Pennsylvania, but it is not George County, the people and places of which are entirely fictitious.

Prologue

It was a dark, moonless, pre-dawn in southwestern Pennsylvania, except for flashes of lightning and the resulting thunder that echoed and rolled across a foggy, night-chilled valley. Some distance away, revealed by lightning flashes one could catch a glimpse of an up-thrust, phallic stone silo attached to what appeared to be the remains of a burned-out barn.

A black van pulled to a stop on a nearby remote gravel road. In the nondescript vehicle, with its mud-spattered license plate, the driver sat in the dark for some time to make sure no one followed or approached. The sound of the engine was replaced by the rumbling thunder in the distance as the driver killed the ignition.

I've never been out here before, this is really the middle of nowhere. I've got to get this over with. The driver pushed a button on the dash releasing the tailgate.

As if signaled by the click, a large black pickup truck pulled within a football field length behind the van and the new arrival turned the engine off. The only sound now was an occasional insect and the distant rumble that rolled down the valley seeming to herald a coming rain.

The truck driver, dressed in black, got out and walked toward the van and slid in on the passenger's side.

"Everything go alright?" asked the van driver.

"I think so. I'm sure glad I had that heavy-duty, trailer-hauling monstrosity back there. I would have never moved that sedan, I pushed on to the rail road tracks, with anything less.

"Yeah," said the driver, "takes a lot of muscle for a job like that. I figure you're pretty strung out, so I'll take care of it from here."

With that, the driver went to the rear of the van, opened the hatch and took out a red and a yellow container. One was gasoline and the other was diesel fuel. The gasoline and an additive would cause a flash fire that would cling to everything and the diesel would assure that the resulting conflagration lasted long enough to consume everything possible.

The two containers were poured over the truck and what remained of the gasoline was poured in a trail toward the van. The driver got back into the van and put the key in the ignition.

"You sure you didn't leave anything?" asked the passenger.

"If you want to be sure about everything, why don't you go check it yourself? I put the gas cans back in and that's all I brought. Did you leave anything?"

"I checked around before I left the truck. It's pretty solid ground so there won't be any tire tracks or footprints. Anyway, it's gonna' rain and wipe everything clean."

The driver started the engine, turned to where the gasoline trail was on the ground, opened the door and leaned out to light the gas trail to what was hoped to be an evidence-erasing inferno.

The passenger turned to look out of the rear window to be sure the fire was doing its job. "Does it for me," was the only comment as the blaze turned the early morning sky a bright orange as a plume of black smoke drifted up into the damp morning air.

"Better get the hell out of here, fast," said the driver, "that sucker is going to draw rubber-neckers like yellow jackets to a cider jug. We'll be hearing about this down at the office for weeks."

A quiet rain began, not heavy enough to affect the fire, but just enough to cover any trace that the couple had been there. The driver and passenger left the truck, the old silo and barn. Turning northward toward the Finger Lakes region of New York as the gas tank exploded carrying a yellow plume high into the air.

Chapter 1

Behavioral Treatments Facility was no Sunnydale home for those with a murderous bent. It wasn't a 19th century snake pit either. From the outside at least, it had he appearance of a college campus, complete with a large administration building and four large dormitories. BTF as it was bureaucratically identified, was in the process of being downsized. The clients housed there wouldn't be released into half-way homes or private treatment centers any time soon. All were there for incarceration as well as treatment. The incarceration part was pretty much it and the treatment part was minimal.

Joey Dulaney found himself exactly where he had planned. Knowing far more than his court-appointed, worthless lawyer. He had, to his mind at least, cleverly managed to be sentenced to a minimum security "hospital" for mentally challenged miscreants and murderers.

Everyone there referred to the place as "The Facility." No one dared use the politically incorrect "prison" or "mental hospital." It housed both genders and several gender-benders of both sexes.

Joey felt he was becoming more and more transparent and that's just what he wanted to be. He wanted people who looked his way to look right through him.

When he first arrived and met his good friend Devon Morrel both could tell Joey was completely opaque. On the outside, "in the world" seeing right through someone meant others could perceive your schemes, your desires, your escape plans. This wasn't the case in, The Facility.

Devon assured him as time passed, if he kept to himself and was passive, he would gradually become more and more transparent until he would become like thin air and no one would even know—or care—that he existed.

"Hell, I've been here for seven years and I'm almost there, completely invisible. I walk around, sometimes where I'm not even supposed to be, and nobody on the staff even notices me—and I'm *black*. You mind yourself, Joey, be a good boy, and you'll get to be invisible real quick. It's a lot easier for white folks—be real easy for you. Tha' homies start pickin' on you, stand up to them, watch yo' ass but don't cause no ruckus, don't get noticed."

* * * *

Getting out would be simple enough since Joey had planned on it since he arrived. He might have fooled the system into buying an insanity plea, but he wasn't crazy enough to wait around until they learned definitely—or differently. He let his hair grow long, keeping it clean and neatly tucked away in a ponytail while blending into the background—becoming ever more transparent. Breaking out was the last thing he considered and he didn't really see his plan as an escape at all.

Escape was something you did from prisons with massive walls and fences and it entailed the risk of being captured, or worse. Breaking out involved tunneling, cutting through bars or killing guards. Walking away was far easier, far more preferable and it sounded a whole lot better too. If you just gave them the slip, they wouldn't look for you too hard, not like if you hurt someone escaping. He'd seen it a hundred times, *"Prisoner Walks Away."* It never got nearly as much attention as *"Prisoner Escapes"* or worse, *Prisoner Kills Guard in Escape Attempt."* An added benefit was, no one on the staff would want to admit that an inmate—whoops—*client* had escaped—whoops—*slipped away*, on their watch.

Inside, the staff felt secure and didn't watch anyone very closely. The staff may have convinced themselves the clients were, too mentally impaired to slip away. They hardly watched the invisible ones at all. Moreover, aside from their valuables, they didn't watch their personal effects very closely either.

* * * *

Early on, Joey had slipped into a changing area and lifted a simple dress from the clothing basket of a female client that looked as if it would fit him. He put it above a ceiling panel in janitor's closet and left. If it was ever missed, no one mentioned it. The staff usually avoided anything that would call attention to themselves, so reporting the theft of a cheap dress would be the last thing anyone would think of doing. They may have thought it was swiped by a transvestite inmate and would, quite naturally, decide to ignore it. Some of the wig pickers might even applaud it as a step toward a client's personal goals fulfillment.

From the beginning, Joey made sure he was closely shaved and because other inmates made him uncomfortably aware he had an androgynous appearance, he knew his plan to slip out as a female staff member or visitor had a chance of success. Admittedly it would be risky, but if caught—well, the staff all agreed he was nuts to begin with.

His therapist insisted he should express himself through drawing and painting so it was easy enough to palm a tube of light red watercolor paint that he could use as lipstick and rouge. He considered swiping a tube of blue for eye shadow, but decided that might be over doing it and the risk wasn't worth the extra effort. He did palm some lamp black to use as eye liner and eyebrow touchup. If no one got a close look, they would never question his disguise. It wouldn't be easy, but if he were careful enough, he could slip out among some of the visitors. He would wear his street clothes under the dress and at the first opportunity, take it off and wipe off his makeup and later cut his hair. Now if he could just get past some of the hornier inmates.

* * * *

The cabin was about eight or more miles from New Vrindavan, (some folks call it New Vrindaban) West Virginia, as the crow flies, but as anyone from George County can tell you, a straight line flown by a crow or any other bird in this part of the country is as rare as a Senator on food stamps.

The two-room shack was almost in West Virginia, close to that part of the state that sticks up between Ohio and the corner stone of the Keystone State. It's called the northern panhandle, but to the new fugitive, he was definitely in Pennsylvania. He was aware that he was in a state that still held the death penalty in reserve for folks like him but just across an imaginary line a few hundred yards away, he could actually murder anyone he wanted to and never be executed for it.

The shack had board and batten siding over a timber frame, the cheapest construction possible and if not for corrugated cardboard boxes held by roofing nails to the inside walls, there would have been no insulation at all. The outside walls were of weathered oak that had never seen paint. It had a corrugated tin roof that the new occupant knew would make it seem even more cozy in a rainstorm. It was undoubtedly a hunter's headquarters, or a dope grower's hideout. This was definitely no Pittsburgh businessman's weekend getaway.

It suited Joey Dulaney just fine. He had hitchhiked several miles, sleeping over in barns for two days and was dropped off in West Finley, north of George County. He was familiar with the area and knew exactly where the shack was. Joey arrived on foot, after a four-mile walk, into what had developed into late evening.

Checking a corroded electrical box near the corner of the house, he found the meter socket empty; undoubtedly the electric company had removed the meter. A quick search and he discovered a length of copper tubing that was easily broken in two to provide jumpers for the electric service. With any luck, the power hadn't been switched off at the transformer on the nearby pole. Using some old inner tube for insulation he jammed the lengths of tubing into place where the meter had been. It might have been more convenient if the meter was in place, but that would also have told him the owners might return at any given moment. Now, he was somewhat relieved knowing that he would be cozy and wouldn't be disturbed for a time.

Inside he found a pallet of rags and old quilts, a nightstand of some sort and best of all, an electrical cube heater. That heater would his salvation. It would keep at least a portion of the cabin warm and there would be no smoke or gas exhaust to betray his presence. If he kept an old, bare bulb lamp shaded well enough, no one would suspect he was anywhere near this part of Pennsylvania. What kind of fool would escape from a mental institution/prison and return to his home county?

A search of a rude kitchen cabinet revealed an assortment of canned goods, some even with labels, and a tin of crackers, food for at least a week. Joey knew there had to be a spring nearby that would provide enough water for his needs. He was able to fall on the pallet of rags, pull a quilt over his hike-tortured body and fall soundly asleep. He was home. He knew there would soon be a manhunt, but they had no idea where to look—for the present.

A breakfast of Vienna sausages, a treat he didn't normally care for, from a pop-open tin and some soda crackers provided a satisfying, if not sumptuous breakfast. It was, as his father told him long ago, a redneck's picnic. Setting the can in front of the heater did little to improve the "tasty" snack, however Joey thought the little piggy peckers never tasted quite so good.

He decided to spend the morning resting up before he undertook a foraging expedition. He knew he'd have to have clothing and if he were particularly lucky, he might acquire a vehicle of some sort. Hopefully, he could steal a car that wasn't being used very often. Not to attract attention, too quickly. So long as he remained out of sight, and didn't move around too much, it would be some time before anyone would know he was in the county.

Later that day, Joey found an empty milk jug and searched for the spring that he knew was near the shack. There had to be a spring or a hand dug well because no one in his right mind would build far away from a water supply. The most likely source would be along the embankment behind the place. His heart beat faster when he found a crude shelter built of cut stone set into the bank. Inside was a spring filled with clear water and because he had spent time on his grandfather's farm in West Virginia, he knew this was an honest to goodness springhouse. The spring flowed into a stone tray and then on downstream. The tray provided a simple cooling system and the chilled interior of the place was just like a refrigerator. *All the comforts of home,* he thought as he filled his jug from the mossy spring and closed the door to the springhouse.

He spent the rest of the day poking around, looking for things he might be able to use for the next few days. Breaking into summer homes and hunting cabins would be easy, but too much of that might call attention to the fact he was in the area, something he would rather avoid. After he had assembled a kitchen knife, some string, some old newspapers and magazines, a hammer with a broken handle and a pencil—he began to take inventory. In addition to clothing, some more food, a razor and toiletries, he would need some cash.

Man, if I could get a rifle, that would be cool. He didn't believe in murder, murder was violent and brutal, he fancied himself civilized, not a brute. The girls who died when he was with them weren't so much murdered; they were eliminated, extinguished or even put down—it was part of his personal gratification ritual. If they were allowed to live, it just wouldn't feel right—he wasn't fulfilled. He knew he couldn't let them be around to tease him about his inadequacies or tell others what he did to them. Besides, the best part was the charge he felt when he killed them.

He'd never killed a man, never even considered it. If he expunged the person who sent him to that nut-house prison, he would have to do it from a distance. That person was a man and men were different because he wasn't a queer. The women he did were for sex, eliminating this deputy sheriff would be for revenge. The pure, sweet, simple, pleasure he felt would be somehow gratifying. Oh yes, gratifying in another way. Eden Whitloe was the prick that found out about him and pretended to be his friend, until the deputy had him put away. Whitloe, he vowed would live to regret it.

Stealing money would raise red flags all over the place. It would have to be done from some distance away from the cabin, so he planned on making his way to Moundsville or perhaps Cameron, the closest towns of any size. Moundsville was larger and he would be less likely to draw attention to himself if he lifted some items or cash from one of its fine establishments, but Cameron was a small town he could easily slip into and out of without making so much as a ripple if he were careful not to call attention to himself. He decided on Cameron.

Chapter 2

Eden Whitloe had been a Deputy for longer than he liked to think about. When Sheriff Oliver Buckey appointed him—unbeknownst to Eden—the appointment was at his father's request. He was fresh out of college and ambitious only to follow the path of least resistance. Employment opportunities for philosophy majors weren't—well, let's say no one was beating down his door with offers. He wasn't detectably ambitious; a major reason the sheriff swore him in as his Deputy. Buckey didn't need some kid with political aspirations snapping at his heels when reelection time rolled around. Whitloe was the perfect Barney Fife for the Sheriff of what might have been—given more southerly climes—Mayberry.

Eden Whitloe's wife Annie died from leukemia less than a year after their wedding ceremony. It was the kind of death that left him with a vast, aching emptiness, and Annie's big orange cat. He didn't quite know how to deal with either of them.

This isn't to infer that Eden wasn't an eligible bachelor—perhaps widower would be a better term. Most women would have considered him a "catch." He was just over six feet tall, average weight and what some might call handsome. He wasn't normally what would be considered imposing, but he had his moments. He was a lawman-cliché and the best description of Eden Whitloe was equally as hackneyed. He was "clean cut," and aside from that, he wasn't a nail that had to be hammered down so it doesn't interrupt the normal flow of traffic. He had all of the ambition of his wife's old tomcat—looking for a place to nap.

Eden was what one might call a utility officer. He did it all and was at the beck and call of his boss, Sheriff Oliver Buckey. His major duties consisted of rounding up bicycle rustlers and folks who drove off without paying for gas at the local stations. He was also the chief part-time enforcement officer for the Grande Place Theater. When he held that august position, his major duty was keeping the homeless from pissing behind the ticket booth. There were restroom facilities right across the street at the George County Courthouse but the homeless eschewed the Courthouse, so at least once a week there was a transgressor or two.

Except for the annual marijuana harvest, George County had just never been a centriole of criminal endeavor. Being rich in George County meant your folks cashed in on natural gas or coal and you could inherit—say a hundred thousand dollars. There just weren't that many rich people to steal from. Not only wasn't there all that much to steal, violence was usually a family affair, limited to the home or taken up at family gatherings.

Except for the bar fight, you couldn't really call murder, that resulted in Don Skomish's early demise at the hands of Fred Schroder, murder was as rare in this part of Pennsylvania as gay weddings. Until the recent co-ed slayings, no murderous events had been reported in the Georgian Observer for several years. Until the "Beautiful Maidens Murder Case," as the press called it, there had been nothing to test the sleuthing skills of Eden Whitloe or Oliver Buckey.

The case would always be problematical for the Deputy because he had actually well, not solved the case, but at least he had closed it. The thing that haunted him was that he knew far more about the four girls' murders than he could reveal to anyone. The case was so involved, so convoluted and confounding that it was impossible to pursue it further. Merely knowing something doesn't make for much of trial, proving it is an entirely different kettle of crap. So far as Eden was concerned, knowing nothing would have been preferable.

Anyway, Joey Dulaney confessed to the "Pretty Maiden" crimes and entered a plea of innocent by reason of insanity. A judge and a battery of psycho-types agreed that he should be put away to protect society and treated until he could stand trial. The judge, the wig-pickers and some other psycho-babblers also agreed he would probably spend the rest of his days growing old, up at the state hospital north of George County. Away from the eyes and minds of George County's voters. They also agreed that God only knew what would happen if he ever came to trial.

The sheriff, who was facing reelection was thrilled at the confessed closure of the matter and rushed to render any further investigation moot. Buckey could have cared less if Jack the Ripper were running amok in his county as long as the voters were happy. He shoved the case file into the far reaches of the farthest filing cabinet.

While he was investigating the Pretty Maiden Murders, Deputy Eden Whitlow worked with a woman who had become his constant obsession and sometime lover. Later he had cause to suspect Shele Ocevan was perhaps a murderer, or at least a conspirator in what he came to believe was a scheme to kill one or more of the college students—or at least cover the killings up. However, as any lawman can tell you, believing or even knowing something is a far cry from getting it on a court docket.

He assumed one of the reasons Shele Ocevan had been murdered was because of her closeness to him. Her car had been forced onto a railroad track and into the path of an oncoming coal train. The incident—or accident, depending on who was telling it

—had happened in the dark of night and no one was sure exactly what occurred. However, the train's engineer told him he thought she was killed when her car was forced into the path of the train by a pickup truck. A stolen truck was later found abandoned and burned by an old barn, for Eden, this was proof enough that Shele had been murdered and the truck was the instrument of her death.

Again, the deputy's beliefs were proof enough for him, but he knew it wouldn't amount to much in the eyes of a judge or jury. He was aware of just enough to make him dangerous to anyone who might have been involved in the killings, but the deputy didn't know enough to seek an indictment.

Eden didn't have much in the way of evidence to present to a sheriff who was up for re-election, but moreover, since he suspected nearly everyone in George County, there was no one, except for Sheriff Buckey, that he trusted to tell about his suspicions. Until the election was over, Buckey would be in no mood to listen and Eden doubted if he would get the sheriff's ear even then.

Belatedly the deputy had checked out Shele Ocevan. He put all of the information he could gather about her into several databases, but turned up essentially nothing. It was as if the name never existed. The only Shele Ocevan he came up with was a name on a passenger ship list from the 1800s. Her Social Security number—or rather the number she gave—belonged to one Bertram Gonslacker of East Pennfield, New York. Evidently Shele was an imposter. If Eden had checked earlier, he might have avoided a world of grief, but he had put off checking up on her for fear of what he might find. He rationalized that he was busy with the investigation and was diverted from his normally cautious approach to this sort of thing. Of course he knew deep down that he was immediately emotionally involved and preoccupied with the strikingly beautiful Miss Ocevan.

Eden felt like he was trapped in an *Invasion of the Body Snatchers* movie. There was no one to be trusted, no one to relate to. He was never as alone as he was when he was thinking of the murders. And when he was at home, alone in his Random Creek home, his thoughts often returned to "The Pretty Maidens."

He did confide in Annie's big orange cat Sarge from time to time but even he seemed distant and suspicious. Eden did, however sometimes feel Sarge was the only one who could be relied upon to keep the information to himself—but he didn't know how far even he could be trusted.

Chapter 3

It was early autumn and Eden was bringing in the last of his tomato harvest. He knew he had only a few short weeks until the first killing frost would ruin the fruits of his summer labors. He also realized the produce was far too bountiful for his own use so he made a mental note to drive over to Brightbrook and leave some tomatoes with his friend Dave Quinn. Dave was an ex-hippie and refugee from the Hare Krishna commune near Moundsville. The two met when Eden enlisted his help when he was investigating the murders. He had almost eliminated Dave entirely from his "suspicious list" but if he never visited anyone on the long list, he might never get out of the house. However, he did try to manage to avoid those on his short list.

After washing the tomatoes and taking a shower, the deputy pulled on a pair of khakis and a plaid shirt—sans underwear and socks—grabbed the day's copy of the Georgian Observer and headed for his back porch swing.

The autumnal equinox had passed and the days were becoming cooler, but a few warm days had lined up and extended the feel of summer for nearly a week. The air was clear, and the last few flies of the season hummed by as Sarge jumped into position on the opposite end of the swing where he prepared for a quick nap. Eden stretched out his legs, put his feet on a low table in front of the swing, opened the paper and began to read. Some distance away he could hear the boom of hunters' shotguns as they practiced for the hunting season that was only a few days away.

Except for his qualms concerning the murders, Eden led an idyllic life on Random Creek. His house sat about a hundred feet from the small stream that ran behind it and about a hundred more feet to the gravel road in front. It was built of recycled materials, old barn board, sash hung windows, and a variety of door styles. The frame was made of timbers from a wagon shed that sat on the property for at least fifty years. The framing was augmented in places, like the back porch, that required more in the way of two-by-four stud construction and more traditional contemporary materials. The house that had been built only a decade ago was in need of a few repairs, repairs that had been put off for some time. The interior was meticulously clean and there were no particular signs of someone who lived a bachelor life. The deputy was a nit-picking housekeeper, just as he was a nit-picking investigator. Possibly the loose ends of the murder case bothered him as much as his reservations about it. Given the chance—a chance that would have involved time off and money—he might have taken up the investigation on his own. Unfortunately, he had been ambitious only to follow the path of least resistance, a path that led to day-to-day work and a deputy's paycheck. His dad had admonished him to find work that he loved and then to make a job out of it. Eden had taken the road most traveled and found a job.

When he heard the sharp crack of a rifle shot, he thought the shot gunner had given up on practicing for small game and picked up a deer gun to sight it in. It was one short report as compared to the constant boom of the shotgun. Gunfire in the western, far reaches, of the county was not at all unusual for this time of the year or about any other time, come to think of it. He probably wouldn't have thought much more of it, except he noticed a small hole in the newspaper he was holding in front of him. He was straightening out the page, getting it into shape for reading the comic section when the shot was fired.

At first it seemed unlikely that it was a bullet hole, but

the appearance of the hole—right in the middle of Hagar the Horrible's helmet—and the report of the rifle, seemed a coincidence worth checking. He looked over his shoulder to the wall of the house behind him. Surely enough there was a small hole in the vinyl siding, perfectly aligned with where the newspaper page had been.

"Damn," Eden said to Sarge, "that was too close. I'm going to ask around tomorrow and see if I can find out who was out here shooting. If I find out who it was, I'll give them a reason to be more careful."

He got up from the swing and Sarge jumped down to join him as both closely examined the hole. He found the bullet had passed through the siding, the sheathing under it and had lodged in one of the two-by-four studs underneath.

Looks like a .30-30, common deer rifle. For a moment he considered digging it out, but realized it would most likely be a futile effort. Even if he did retrieve the bullet and it was in good enough condition for ballistics, what would he do with the information? He surely couldn't track down every deer rifle in the tri-state region to see if the gun owner's rifle matched the missile.

"What do you make of it?" he asked the big orange cat, who cocked his head inquisitively.

He also quickly dismissed the fleeting notion that the shot had been an intentional attempt on his life. He remembered when some hunter had shot Joe Bill Tusten—mistaking him for a squirrel—and quickly dismissed the thought. Accidental gunshots killed far more people in the rural areas of Pennsylvania than intentional ones. Unfortunately, his rational, lawman brain took over his intuitive analysis of the incident.

Got to be careful about this sort of thing, he said to himself, too damned easy to fall into paranoia living out here alone.

At the same time, Sarge meowed loudly. "Oh, I'm sorry," Eden said, "I guess I'm not alone." Sarge rubbed his big orange head against the deputy's leg and Eden stooped to scratch him

26

behind his ears.

It was a day that convinced the deputy that it might be the last gasp of summer-like weather. Cornfields were brown rows of stubble dotted with shocks awaiting homes to decorate and Halloween parties to visit. The first leaves of autumn were losing their grip and suicidal chipmunks romped the road daring him to help them avoid the winter misery to come. Eden loaded a peck basket of tomatoes in his 1999 model pickup and made his way across the steep ridge in front of his house to Brightbrook.

It was a small enough village with only about twenty-five inhabitants, when they were all at home. To further reduce the winter population, a handful of residents would leave for sunnier weather to the south where they would frolic until spring. Dave Quinn claimed the village was so small the state could have saved money by painting the entering and leaving Brightbrook notices on the same sign.

Dave owned and operated a cabinet making and furniture shop in what would have been the suburb of town—if there had been a town. Actually he was on the leading and following edge of the tiny community. His shop, also his home, was fashioned from what remained of a '50s Art Deco filling station. He had salvaged most of it and the garage served as his work area while the store part of the station was his home. One of those chrome monstrosity booths from the '50s—complete with a jukebox selector connected to nothing—served as his breakfast nook.

To Eden's way of thinking, the place fit Dave Quinn to a 'T'. It was everything one might expect. You see Dave was a 1960's free spirit of the '69 *Easy Rider* vintage. Eden thought of him as a Dennis Hopper simile, but he was undoubtedly more of the Luke Askew variety—if the deputy had been up on his Rider filmography.

27

When Eden arrived he found a relatively new BMW sitting out front, beside Dave's delivery truck. The two trucks looked like an old pair of work boots on each side of the patent leather Beamer between them. He hesitated to intrude further, but knew the tomatoes wouldn't last out the week if he took them home. He was determined to at least drop them off, so he went to the front door to knock. At about the time he decided to go around to the side door, Dave appeared in the doorway to answer his knock.

"Hey, it's Eden—what's-his-name," he said with a big grin, full knowing it was Deputy Eden Whitloe. "Come on in— stranger."

"I'm not interrupting anything," Eden said, nodding toward the new car out front.

"Oh, no. That's a customer's car. "We were just closing a deal on a couple of pieces I made recently. We're done dealing now. Come on in and I'll introduce you. Too young for me," he said in a stage whisper behind his hand.

Chapter 4

Eden fully expected to be introduced to one of the gay Pittsburgh designers Dave was always talking about, so the introduction to Miss Alna Byrne came as a welcome surprise. "Miss Byrne," said Dave, "this is the famous George County Deputy Sheriff and Chief Investigator you must have heard about.

Eden, this is Alna Byrne a designer for Favregiano's Furnishings in Upper Saint Claire."

Eden couldn't help noticing the emphasis on the Miss part of the introduction.

Alna Byrne looked to be in her late twenties—twenty-nine was the number that would have been revealed by the date of birth on her driver's license if Eden had picked her up for speeding. She was dressed in a typical designer's uniform, low-cut jeans and a blouse with a sweater worn like a neck scarf. (Eden saw this as a yuppie-ism and always thought it was stupid.) She wore clear fingernail polish, muted lipstick and minimal eye-makeup for blue-gray eyes that wouldn't have been improved by it. Her honey blonde hair hung in ringlets as if it had just been released from restrictive braids and on top of her head, were a pair of designer sunglasses. (Bvlgari was a name Eden wouldn't have recognized, if he had wanted to.) Eden assumed, correctly, that this was another element of the designer motif and found it additionally annoying. In any event, the overall effect was stunning. Not that Alana

29

Byrne was drop-dead gorgeous by any means, she just used everything she had to its fullest.

Shele Ocevan, the deputy's late assistant was strikingly beautiful and his late wife, Annie had been simply pretty in the best sense of the word. Miss Byrne was somewhere in between. Women of the Ocevan ilk made him feel inadequate, bumbling and he always felt, no, not felt—*was*—tongue-tied around them. He knew he would be far more comfortable with the attractive, but less than drop dead gorgeous, Miss Byrne.

"I was just about to pour some coffee, you take yours black don't you?" asked Dave.

"I brought over some tomatoes…"

"You and everybody else around here—I'm sorry, it's not that I don't appreciate the thought, but Colleen McKay dropped off a bushel yesterday. You remember her from up in Amity?"

"Yeah, how's she doing? I—uh—I suppose I could take them…"

"Oh no, you're not taking them back. I'll throw them in with the rest. I've got a pot—no a kettle—going on a hot plate back in the finishing room. I'll cook them down, then make catsup or pasta sauce out of them later."

"I had no idea you were a chef, I'm going to have to invite myself back for dinner," said Alna.

"You know you're welcome anytime. You keep buying the stuff I make and I'll feed you every time you come by. Ah, that's '*buy*' with a 'u' between the 'b' and 'y'."

"Eden's a pretty decent cook. I know he doesn't look like much, but he makes a dandy breakfast—burns the pancakes once in a while though."

"Eden—Eden Whitloe. Hey," said Alna, "I think I read somewhere that you caught up with the guy that killed those girls. Now I remember, I thought the name Eden Whitloe sounded familiar. Here I am discussing how the famous detective burns pancakes. I *am* impressed."

Eden stopped himself from doing an audible, aw shucks, and returned what might have seemed like a grimace rather than the smile he intended.

"He was some kind of nut-bar, perverted killer wasn't he?"

"Still is, I reckon, put him up near Pittsburgh in a hospital for the criminally disturbed. Anyway he confessed to the killings and he'll be there for the rest of his days—or until he becomes sane again. I think that's pretty doubtful though. I think his chain has definitely slipped its sprocket."

"His name is Joey Dulaney and Eden here has other suspicions about the case, don't you Eden?" said Dave.

Eden frowned to let Dave know he didn't want to discuss it. "I don't know, just seems like there should be more to it," he fumbled. "We spent all that time doing an investigation and then he just up and puts the whole thing away, too neat for me I guess."

"I agree with the investigator," said Dave. "There was an unexplained suicide and what looks to have been another—"

"Let's talk about it another time," interrupted Eden. "It's all too morbid for this fine day. Alna, Dave says you bought some things; you need help loading anything into the car?"

"I'm going up her way in a few days," said Dave, "so she won't be taking anything with her. You can help me put them in the delivery van later if you like."

"It's awfully sweet of you to offer Eden," Alna said with a gracious smile. "Maybe when I get down here next month, I can maneuver a breakfast invitation—if you promise not to burn the pancakes."

"You don't have to maneuver anything, you've got a deal. And, I only overly-brown my pancakes when I'm trying to get rid of someone who is a pain in the ass," he gave Dave a scorching glance. "In your case, the cooking will be watched and the pancakes will be done to perfection."

"I'll make a note to not become a pain in the ass," she said with a seductive smile. "Can I have permission to talk about the murder case when we next meet? Dave really has my curiosity aroused now. I thought the whole thing was settled over a year ago."

"I don't want to make too much of it being unsettled, it's pretty much over with—just a couple of troubling things about it that's all. I'll tell you all about it in a very, very short time when we meet for breakfast," Eden pushed her. "You want to set a time?"

Eden was anxious to see how deep her interest was. He suspected she was more interested in him than the case, and now his curiosity was really piqued.

"Hey, let's go back to the shop and I'll show you what Alna selected. It's only a few select pieces." Dave interrupted.

Moving toward a set of glazed, double doors, Eden and Alna, were led by Dave to what used to be the garage section of the old gas station. Dave turned to close the doors, "Keeping those closed is important. The whole house begins to smell like linseed oil and turpentine if I don't keep them shut."

"Walnut?" said Eden. "This isn't…"

"Yes it is," replied Dave, "it's part of that old stump you helped me dig up in barter for your back-porch swing."

"It's more than I ever imagined," Eden said, rubbing his hand across the figured grain. "It's absolutely gorgeous. The way you booked the burls, it looks like a Rorschach test. The hands of the master—"

"Hmm," murmured Alna. "What do you see in there? I always see bats and butterflies."

"Those things always looks like a OBGYN study to me," Eden said, checking to see if anyone blushed.

"Very intres-tink," said Dave in his best impression of an Austrian Psychiatrist. "Now I know I'm dealing with a sex fiend."

"Hey, you're the guy that makes the dirty 'pitchures' outa wood," Eden said, with a laugh.

Chapter 5

Oliver Buckey had been the sheriff of George County Pennsylvania for over two decades. He was sheriff long before his deputies Eden Whitloe, Arleigh and Junior Slaughter were appointed. Arleigh and Junior were Darryl and Darryl bookend Bubbas. *Seems like the rurals around here have always had bubba names*, Eden thought. He was never quite sure of the relationship Arleigh and Junior had with Buckey although he thought he heard they were second cousins. But then, who in George County wasn't a second or third cousin of someone, or everyone. There were several family trees in which Eden wasn't too sure about their branches.

The sheriff swore Eden in almost ten years ago over the objection of another cousin who had his eye on the job. He and Buckey had recently gone through what Buckey hoped would be his last election campaign and things were almost back to normal. As it turned out, the murders weren't even a factor in the vote. Surprisingly, the lucky sheriff along with his crew ran unopposed.

"Just call me Buckey," was his tagline, campaign slogan. He once admitted to his Deputy that he never liked his first name, "Oliver." He thought it sounded—well—it just wasn't an electable name for a Sheriff. Buckey felt his full name sounded like he should be selling farm equipment or could he could be taken for an undertaker.

Oliver Buckey looked the part of Sheriff. He wore dark

Men In Black reflector shades and he had a waist for the job. An overhang above a belt that he cinched somewhere near the tops of his thighs fully fulfilled the promise of his one-horse town sheriff's image. His huge brass western belt buckle disappeared somewhere between the top of his trousers and his shirt. Sheriff Buckey had the name and look of a rural lawman and Eden didn't.

Buckey secretly told Eden that he didn't intend to run again and that the deputy should be getting his act together for a run for the office if he wanted to keep his job and maintain any sort of pension. He assured him that neither Junior nor Arleigh wanted the job; they just wanted to be deputies. Evidently they were wise men, they knew the limits of their combined intellect.

Right then and there Eden began to think about an electable nickname. He rejected more than two-dozen and never did find one that was suitable. *Anyway, four years should be enough time to come up with something that might work.* He already felt exhausted, just having to think about running a campaign. He always thought of himself as just being along for the ride. Do what you're told; keep your head down and out of your ass and keep your job was, he firmly believed, the sure formula to retirement with a pension.

Aside from Dave Quinn, Buckey was one of the few that were on the list of those he trusted. He felt his old friend would be at his back come hell or high water and the reason he thought so was that on at least a couple of occasions, he had turned around and Buckey was there, backing him up. He had never had a reason to doubt his old friend, an old comrade he trusted with his very life.

Still Eden hadn't made his reservations concerning the murders known to Buckey. The end of the case had come at the beginning of the campaign and there was no reason to muddy the waters, that had been cleared for the electorate. The voters were satisfied, and if Eden had revealed what he suspected, it might have not only have hurt the chances of his friend being re-elected, it might have cost him his job. He told himself there would be time enough for him to reveal everything later and he desperately wanted to dump everything in the sheriff's lap and let him deal with the ramifications of it.

* * * *

Sheriff Buckey had returned late that afternoon from an appointment with the doctor.

"You gonna live?" asked Eden. "I'd try to stay away from Dr. Vinnie if I were you.

"I went to see that new Indian doctor name of Sharan, I think. I haven't been feeling up to snuff lately, so I thought I'd get a checkup. Did the blood tests, EKG, even the old finger wave."

"So, what did you find out?"

"I have the doctors permission to live through the next term of office. After that, I might have to turn the whole thing over to you.

"You using your pickup tomorrow afternoon?" Buckey asked.

"Why? You ain't takin' Kathy Robinson out to the state park again, are you?"

"Now don't go pissin' me off. You know how that shit gets me riled when you get it started. You know very well I had to take her out there on business."

"Bet it got Mr. Robinson riled too," Eden said, enjoying Buckey's discomfort. The deputy really didn't know what happened out at the state park, but he jerked him around about it as a joke once and when Buckey rose to the bait he knew he had struck a nerve—pay dirt.

"Nuthin' happened," Buckey protested—too much. "If you're going to be an asshole about it, you can keep your damned truck and I'll take a squad car—get a trailer."

"Aw Buckey, don't be mad at me," he could see the sheriff cooling off. "You can use it all you like. "Just make sure you clean the pecker tracks off the seat," he added, just to ice the cake.

With that, the sheriff picked up a notebook from his desk and hurled it at the deputy, making sure it didn't come anywhere near him as he headed for the door.

"Hey Buckey," Eden shouted. Buckey turned to face him. The deputy tossed him a key ring, "don't forget the keys."

A few seconds after Buckey left, Arleigh Slaughter walked in.

"Hey Eden, will you stay late and cover for me? I got to pick something up and it's going to take a while. What's eatin' Buckey? He didn't even say hi, just walked by like he was in a snit or something."

"Oh, he just borrowed my truck to haul something out to his place in the western end. You know I have to jerk him around when he borrows anything. Nothing personal, I just pissed him off, that's all. Don't you just love it?" said Eden with a devilish grin. "Go ahead, I'll be here a while anyway."

* * * *

Eden was left to his own resources. It was late afternoon; no one was around the tomb-like office. Even the receptionist had taken the afternoon off. The only sound was a ticking time clock and the seldom noticed—until now—gurgle of the old boiler pipes coming from somewhere under the floor.

He settled into his antique oak swivel chair. He rescued it from the dumpster. Although it wasn't as comfortable as the padded monstrosity that was provided by the county, it had character. It had that solid, Sam Spade feel to it. When Eden was alone within his thoughts his imagination slipped to film noir, *Maltese Falcon* and *The Big Sleep*. He was Philip Marlow in his oak chair, his computer keyboard was an Underwood and his 9mm automatic was a hefty 38. Snub-nose revolver in a shoulder holster. His name on his office door would be lettered on frosted glass in gold leaf and outlined in black. That was when investigative work had style; it was a time when he could have been somebody instead of…

He was jolted from his reverie by rap on the door.

It was Elvira Gulch, right out of *The Wizard of Oz*. Well, not really, but she looked a lot like Margaret Hamilton to Eden.

"Oh sheriff," she began. From there on the best he could make out was that some boy had run his bicycle into her rose trellis and her prize flowers had been ruined. Telling her the growing season was over did nothing to calm her. She insisted the matter be thoroughly investigated and the culprit apprehended, tried, convicted — and shot. Eden suppressed a desire to ask, are you a good witch or a bad witch, in his best Billie Burke voice.

It was just the sort of annoying incident that the deputy could never admit to enjoying. He knew this was a sign his life and that of his town, Rainelle, in general was back to normal. A recent complaint from Reverend Dave Bruester concerning the town's lady of the evening, the sixty-something Sheila Liebeck, gave him further assurance that things were back in their usual rut — ah, groove. And, the reverend's passing gripe about "the goings-on" at Lin Kelley's Saloon gave him even more comfort.

"Well, Mrs. Welchner, do you have any idea where I should begin?" Eden asked, just for the hell of it. (He had no intention of doing anything.)

"How should I know, I'm not an officer of the law, duly sworn to uphold it. If I were you, I'd start with looking for one of the kids who is missing a bicycle. He left it in my trellis, so I locked it up in my garage."

"I'll look into it," he assured her. He knew this would be only the opening round of another feud between Mrs. Welchner and the neighborhood kids and decided to try his best to stay out of it for as long as possible.

After Mrs. Welchner departed, Eden turned down the annoying two-way radio and renewed his swivel chair position. He looked across this desk and the neat freak in him broke out as he began to straighten all the folders and to discard the discardables. His compulsive side emerged and he arranged all of the desk items in order around his blotter. Of course no one used the desk protector as a blotter anymore and the desktop was marred far beyond any need of protection. He paid little attention to the clock, which was indicating a few minutes after 7:30 and he had barely noticed the fading light. He had nowhere in particular to go and all of his investigative tasks were done for the day. He resumed his pre-Welchner position and his interrupted *Big Sleep* fantasy.

Just about the time Bogie (Marlow/Eden) was being taunted by Bacall (Vivian/Alna), "So you're a private detective. I didn't know they existed, except in books," he was jolted from his fantasy by the scream of distant sirens.

Chapter 6

In most towns, even small towns, the sound of sirens wouldn't get much of a passing notice. In Rainelle, Pennsylvania, the sound of sirens struck fear in the heart of every mother who just knew her children were being carted off to George County Memorial, or worse, the morgue and Walbridge's Funeral Home. In Rainelle, emergency vehicles were seldom used and when they were, the drivers usually relied on their vehicle's horn to warn pedestrians and traffic out of their path. The volunteer firemen did take particular delight in turning on their screaming klaxons and in using their intersection-air-horns, but they were distinguishable from the ambulance/police variety.

Eden and everyone in town knew that something was terribly wrong. The last time anyone could remember hearing such a commotion was when the Sapphire Coal Mine had exploded. He turned the radio squelch off and cranked the volume up.

In the background noise he thought he heard "Code thirty—noise—officer down, buzzing sound—help emergency! "Ten-seventy one" (the code for a shooting,) "Ten-forty nine, ambulance needed" followed by what he thought was a "Ten-forty five D, static," and a disheartening "Ten-thirty six, whistle and buzzing," (confidential information.) "All units report."

* * * *

Knowing the phone lines were likely to be tied up Eden started off for the parking lot. Before he got to the door, he suddenly remembered Buckey had taken his pickup and he needed the keys to the squad car or the SUV. Emerging from the office, he located Buckey's big old Buick squad car that made him think of the old black and white TV show, *Highway Patrol* and one of his film noir favorites, Broderick Crawford. The Crawford jowls reminded him of Dr. Vinnie.

He got into the car and sat there trying to figure out what to do next. He was sure he had to do something, but now he'd made it to the car, he wasn't quite sure what to do, where to go. *If only Buckey were here, he'd know what to do.*

He tried the car's two-way and found, like much of the county's equipment, it didn't work. Thinking, the "officer down" was one of the state troopers making a fatal traffic stop on the Interstate, he tried his cell phone. Only two bars, whom to call? Maybe Arleigh or Junior—hell, maybe one of them was the officer down. Buckey was out in the country picking up God knows what in his pickup and sure to be far from any cell and safe from trouble. He couldn't seem to concentrate; his thoughts were coming as if he was a speed freak or a manic giving full reign to a meth-modified mind.

He picked Arleigh out of his contacts menu and pushed "send."

"Hello… breakup… hello?" said Arleigh.

"It's me, Eden," he said. "You got any idea what all the ruckus is about?"

"Don't know, I'm headed toward the west end and there's losta' traffic headed this-a-way. I'll stop someone and see if I can find out. I'll call you back when I learn something and get to the top of a hill and improve my signal."

It was only a few minutes but it seemed like hours. Eden was always startled when his cell phone rang. He had the thing turned up to its loudest and most annoying setting because he hated missing calls and having to check his voice mail.

"This is Slaughter again," said the distant voice. "I'm coming up on top of the ridge out here and things should improve. Can you hear me now?"

"Yes," Eden said impatiently. "I can hear you real good."

"You ain't hurt are you?"

"WHAT!"

"I thought you said…"

"Yes! I can hear you good, I just don't know what you mean by am I hurt."

"I stopped Pam Bleeker and she said she heard you was the one that wrecked. Said everyone out that way knows your pickup and they was hauling it in to Scotty McMillan's. She said it was a real mess and they were hauling your ass outa there in an ambulance."

"Oh my God Arleigh, Buckey borrowed my truck. It has to be him in that wreck. Get to the hospital and see what you can find out. I'll meet you there."

Eden put the Buick in drive and headed for George Memorial with his siren now adding to the confusion and clamor of the others. When he arrived, he couldn't get near the place. There were State Police cars and official vehicles of every description in the parking lot. Many of the drivers were walking back to their cars as he arrived. Arleigh Slaughter was nowhere to be seen and now TV satellite trucks were starting to swarm in. Eden knew it had to be something bad, really bad.

He pulled into a fire lane and stopped Dan Brackenridge, the head of the State Police. Dan had his head down and seemed to be in a sort of daze.

"I'm sorry Eden…" he choked back a sob.

"It's Buckey isn't it? He's—dead—don't tell me Buckey's dead."

"I'm sorry…"

"How'd it happen? Oh Lord it was my truck he was driving…"

"Nuthin' to do with your truck Eden, nuthin' like that,"

Dan assured him. "Some son-of-a-bitch shot him and he ran off the road. He was probably dead before he went over the guide rail. Shot him right through the front windshield, through the head. Never knew what hit him, never had a chance." Brackenridge, the tough cop who had seen it all, sort of collapsed into his car, put his head on the steering wheel and simply wept.

The struck-dumb deputy stood there feeling as useless as he had ever felt in his life. Hot tears were streaming down his cheeks, but they weren't so much tears of sorrow as they were steaming tears of anger—futile, powerless rage.

"I wish it had been me," he mumbled.

"What?" asked Brackenridge?

"He never did anything to deserve—this—this… I said, I wish it had been me instead of Buckey."

Dan looked up from the steering wheel and with a look that Eden would take to his grave said, "Eden, I think that's exactly what the shooter had in mind."

Chapter 7

At first the only evidence was the truck. Later, after the initial autopsy, the bullet was recovered from the truck and examined. Not clean enough to match with a similar bullet; it had smashed into the rear of the truck cab. It was a soft-nosed slug and was so distorted not much could be determined from it. Dr. Vinnie, who had performed the autopsy, offered the opinion that it could be from a .30-30 caliber rifle. He callously offered, "Makes a good deer gun if you want to be sure you kill 'em with one shot." Sensitivity was never Dr. Vinnie's strong suit.

Hell, it could have been from the same rifle that barely missed Eden earlier in the week. It occurred to him that it might be worthwhile to dig that one out and see if the two were from the same rifle. Eden would cut into his wall and remove four inches of the stud in which the bullet was lodged and send it to the state ballistics lab. The slug they recovered wasn't much more than a mushroomed lump and except for the fact it was a familiar round, it was essentially useless.

An analysis of the path of the bullet revealed that Buckey had been shot from a position high on a hilltop. Without knowing the precise location of the truck at the time the bullet struck, there was no way to determine the shooter's exact position. A subsequent search of the hillside, revealed nothing more than a candy wrapper that could have blown in or been left there by anyone.

Although there was an outside chance it was an accidental shooting, Eden and the other law enforcement officers were convinced it was an intentional attempt to assassinate the George County Sheriff—or perhaps his deputy.

"I can't live here in the office and no amount of body guards are going to protect me, what am I going to do," Eden asked Dan Brackenridge.

"Only one thing you can do. Find the bastard and get him first."

"Can't figure why anyone out there would want me dead," said Eden.

* * * *

Weeks passed without further incident giving Eden hope that the assassin had been scared off by all of the attention the death of the sheriff had focused on the county, but he was afraid that sooner or later another attempt would be made. The question was could he track the shooter down before he struck again?

Eden walked around in a daze. It was bad enough losing a close friend, but believing he was under a death sentence took its toll as well. The deputy suffered from what some might call paranoia, not the delusional kind but a very logical suspicion of nearly everyone in town. Even before the shooting incidents, he had good reason to suspect more than a few of the local businessmen.

To add to his burden, the judge insisted he assume the office of sheriff, at least until the next election.

"Hell no Neale, I can't do it. I'm not cut out to be the boss. I ain't no leader," he told the Judge.

"I know you well enough to know what you can do better than you do. I'm not giving you a choice. There's no one more qualified, so it's settled and done with. Raise your right hand."

"Right here and now? Don't I get a chance to think about it? Don't I get to—to nominate someone else? You make me sheriff and I'll have to talk someone into doing *my* job."

Judge Neale Canfield was determined. "Raise your right hand. Do you solemnly swear?"

"Aren't you supposed to use a Bible or something?"

Without a Bible or further ado Deputy Eden Whitloe became the Sheriff of George County.

"Now Sheriff," said Canfield, "go out and find yourself a deputy."

* * * *

The newly appointed sheriff almost said, who in the hell would take a shit job like that? But his mind was already racing ahead. Buckey was the only one he completely trusted and about everyone else in town was, he believed, somehow involved in the killings of the girls. And, he believed either the same person who shot Buckey or someone connected with the other murders took him out. The only thing that made sense was, one of the members of the cult that he had uncovered during his investigation of the killings intended to add him to the body count.

He trusted Lin Kelley, but she wouldn't be much help and wouldn't leave the saloon where she provided much-needed community social work and more importantly, she served as a highly reliable source of information. Lin Kelley could keep nothing to herself. It seemed all of the folks he felt he could depend on were either too old or incompetent to become lawmen. And, he wouldn't enlist the aid of another assistant without vetting them thoroughly—this time.

The only name that survived on his short list was Dave Quinn. Dave was a little long in the tooth, but Eden had seen him wrestle a huge stump out of the ground and didn't think he would want to tangle with him. *I'll just invite that gentleman over for breakfast.*

He spent the evening and all of the next day running background checks on David Hayes Quinn, a.k.a. Raghunatha from his Hare Krishna days. The sheriff simply couldn't believe his eyes, no criminal record, not even a traffic ticket.

During the '60s, he checked Dave's experiment in Hinduism and the "hippie years," no drug busts, no DUI, no nothing. His financials were clean; he missed a utility bill or two, but that was about it. Eden even got into his medical files because he wanted to know if Dave had messed his head up at some point. He didn't want to be holding the hand of a lithium muncher or a closet drug addict. The only thing about Dave's past that concerned him was the fact that he was so squeaky clean—not at all what one would expect of an old fart, ex-hippie—a closet square.

The question was whether to drop in, or call to arrange a meeting. Calling would forewarn him and give him time to prepare an argument for refusing to help out. It would be best to sort of sneak up on him, lay a trap and see if he would rise to the bait. Already Eden was feeling queasy about the whole thing. Did he want to consider a deputy who really didn't want the job?

He knew his work was cut out for him. Dave had a lucrative business going full tilt and seemed satisfied with where he was in life. He certainly wasn't an audacious youngster who might be looking for excitement and adventure and perhaps that was an advantage.

Hell, he's a few years older but he's pretty much like me, an old tomcat looking for a place to take his next nap.

Discarding the idea of calling first, Eden made the trip to the Brightbrook furniture/cabinet shop one more time to request the presence of David Quinn at the home of Sheriff Eden Whitloe for the purpose of partaking in a breakfast meal. He didn't give a hint of the real purpose of the invitation, and he had every reason to believe Dave didn't either. Eden left without explaining anything about the breakfast meeting. "Gotta' run," he said. "I have to be back at the office in fifteen minutes."

The morning started over orange juice and before they switched to coffee, Dave began the conversation. "I'll bet now you've got a big promotion and are making the big bucks, you want to buy some original Quinn furnishings to match your porch swing?"

"Is that something that came from probing the infinite — you been using your omniscient powers again?" Dave was a sometime psychic that Eden employed after he and Buckey became desperate in their investigation of the multiple murders.

"Well, do you want to buy some furniture?"

"I've been thinking about it," Eden fibbed.

"Maybe I got the wrong 'impression,' let me cogitate once more. I may have to consult with the other side."

"As full of it as ever," chided Eden. He was convinced Dave was sensitive and picked up on body language quickly, but he never did put much faith in psychics — particularly after he had consulted a few of them.

"Wait, it's becoming clearer. I can feel it... ah — um, you are here for something. This isn't just a friendly visit to pass the time of day — you have something in mind. What the hell do I smell burning?"

"Pancakes!" Eden shouted, running for the stove. He grabbed the cake turner and deftly stepped on the treadle to open the waste can and flipped the now blackened flapjacks into it, letting the lid slam shut."

"Was that to indicate my status as an asshole?" Dave grinned.

"You're the omniscient all-seeing one, you tell me."

"I'll do it," He exclaimed exuberantly.

"What the hell? What will you do?"

"Be your deputy, you dumb ass."

"Alright, don't give me a pants load of that 'probing the infinite' crap, Professor Marvel. Just what the hell makes you think I'm going to ask you to be my deputy?"

"Simple. Everyone in town knows you have to get a replacement for yourself and you have to do it quickly. And, you have to find out whoever it is that's after your ass. Right?"

Eden hated to admit it. "Yes but…"

"Well, now Dudley," he said using the name of the cartoon Mounty, Shele Ocevan, had always kidded him about. "Who else ya' got?"

Eden replied sheepishly, "Nobody. Will you do it?" he implored.

"Hey, where were you a few seconds ago? I just said I'd do it."

"It's a shit job. I can tell you from personal…"

"Hell Eden, I know that; I know nobody else would touch the job with a ten-foot pole if they had half a brain. Oh, don't worry; no way I'm making it a lifetime endeavor. I'll do it until we catch whoever killed Buckey, then as Johnny Paycheck was wont to say, you can take your job and shove it."

"You sure? No strings? No if, ands or buts?"

"Just one thing."

"Yeah, there's always just one more thing. Go ahead, drop the other shoe."

"I want Alna Byrne to help out—kinda' like Shele did—if that's okay with you."

Eden looked at his prospective deputy with more of a smirk than a grin. "Look, if you knew half as much as I do about Shele Ocevan, you'd never say you wanted someone to help out the way she did. And remember, whatever she was doing got her killed—at least the way I've got it figured."

"I'm not dissuaded at all, I still…"

"You're trying to fix me up, aren't you?"

"Not really," Dave protested. "Alna's got some pretty uncanny abilities, and not in the department you're thinking about—you dirty old man. She was a reporter for a TV station over in Youngstown and has a lot of investigative experience. You want a background check done; she's right up there with the best. I'm not asking you to employ her or pay her or anything like that. Just let her help out from time to time.

Nothing even semi-permanent."

"I should have my head examined," said Eden. "If you agree to serve as deputy—until we find who killed Buckey—and if you agree to be responsible for Miss Byrne—shows you how desperate I am..."

"It's a deal," interrupted Dave. "Swear me in, let's get started."

"Not so fast, I don't even know who's supposed to do it and what all's involved. I'll have to check with Judge Canfield on it. Don't get in such a big rush."

"Hey, buddy, you're the one that should be in a rush. I think there's someone out there who wants you dead, and after I muck around in the case for a while, they may even rush the job. Hell, they might get interested in me. Let's find the bastard as quickly as we can." Dave sounded far more enthusiastic than Eden felt.

Chapter 8

Judge Neale Canfield held the ceremony right in the George County Courtroom. This time he made Dave hold up his hand and put the other one on a bible—held by Sheriff Eden Whitloe—while standing in front of the State Seal. It was for public consumption and press relations. The judge practically sent out a summons for the Georgian Observer's photographer to be there. He wanted everyone to know it was an official photo op sanctioned by the court.

The affair afterward couldn't be called a reception, but Eden arranged a gathering of the office staff and some of the State Police so he could introduce the new deputy and get everything off to a good start. At one point, Arleigh Slaughter took Eden to one side and asked about Dave's age.

"He's only going to be around for a short time, until we catch whoever did Buckey. Don't worry so much, you have a secure job here—unless you screw up," Eden told him. He added the tag, just to keep Arleigh on his toes.

"Long as I don't have to pull the old geezer's load," agreed Arleigh.

As the party wound down, Eden sought out the new deputy and asked him to step into his office.

"I'd like to get together with you and Alna as soon as possible, we need to be sure we're all on the same page." He wanted to share what he had learned about the killings while both of them were present.

I ran a background check on Miss Byrne and except for a couple of traffic tickets, she seems to be all she appears to be," he told Dave. He wanted Dave to know, a pretty face and a smile didn't impress him. At least they didn't impress him anymore.

"I'll bet you ran a deep, deep, check on me," said Dave.

"Hey I even dug into the Old Ex-hippie Fart files and there you were," he kidded his new deputy. "Anyway, you think you guys can make it this weekend, say Saturday for lunch?"

"What about breakfast?"

"There's some folks who can't handle my breakfasts."

"Okay," said Dave, "I know when I'm whipped. I'll make sure both of us are there—for lunch."

* * * *

Winter was only weeks away on Random Creek and the air had a bite that carried small flakes of snow. Only a few oaks were holding onto their leaves with a death grip that would soon loosen leaving only the hangers on that soon would be loaded with snow.

Fifteen minutes before noon, Alna and Dave arrived, hung their coats on an antique hall tree and took their places at the kitchen table. Eden busied himself at the stove, stirring pots, adjusting burners, and adding things he took from an overhead cabinet.

"Need any help over there sheriff?" asked Alna.

"Not right now. Maybe after lunch you can talk Dave into doing the dishes," he replied.

They all knew it was an empty threat because they could see the kitchen was equipped with a dishwasher. The meal went quietly enough as everyone exchanged small talk. No one seemed ready to broach the subject of how they got to where they were, or how they were to proceed. The meal ended with everyone helping to clear the table and put the dishes in the sink. Eden poured sodas and put out some cookies as they retired to the living room.

"Don't get too relaxed, we have a lot to accomplish today. We may be here for a while and you might want to take notes," Eden began. "Alna, I assume Dave has told you most of what he knows about the case."

Alna nodded as Eden went on to explain how he and Buckey were investigating the disappearance of Myra Kinchloe and how Dave became involved in the case.

"Buckey and I got bogged down initially and with no clues or any evidence. So, we contacted what turned out to be one of Dave's colleagues. Amara McClure was a local psychic and we had hopes that she could at least give us some direction—some idea of where to start.

"As you may know," he said, directing his attention to Alna, "McClure shot herself... uh... anyway, according to the reports it was a suicide. Next, more young women, including the missing Myra Kinchloe were turning up dead in the game lands out on the western end of the county."

Eden related how Joey Dulaney became a person of interest when he found the tires on his van matched the plaster casts that had been taken at one of the murder scenes. With that piece of evidence, things moved along quickly and eventually Joey was arrested. He eventually confessed to the murders.

"End of story, right? Well, not quite. I was never convinced that Joey killed all of the girls. I always suspected he killed one or two of them but at least one... well; I'll get into that in time. So, to keep things straight, we have five dead women, the four girls and Amara McClure who I was never convinced committed suicide."

"More soda anyone? I'll get it," said Alna.

Both men refused and Eden continued to sum up the story.

"As I said, Shele Ocevan, who was supposedly McClure's niece, shows up with a couple of people who are passed off as McClure's friends. She and the friends are there to take care of funeral arrangements and clean up the estate."

Eden told them, as he found out later, none of them were

who they claimed to be. He had attempted to run traces on them and turned up nothing. None were related to McClure and after Shele Ocevan, or whoever she was, was killed; the other two disappeared into the woodwork.

"Oh yes, there was a friend of Shele's who ostensibly came down to George County to help in the investigation. She disappeared after Shele's death and there is no trace of her either. It's like four people came out of nowhere and three returned from whence they came."

"Norma and Eric Strohman, Aingeal Farrell whoever they were, said they were returning to upstate New York. Eden had no idea if Norma and Eric were actually married and no clue if any of the three even knew Amara McClure before she died. Limited resources on this end prevented us from going up there for a full-blown investigation."

"Like the man says," began Dave, "ya' can't tell the players without a program. Well now we know their names—maybe not who they are—but we know some names."

Chapter 9

"I'll tell you what I suspect happened. There's still a lot of blanks to be filled in and we'll get into this more later," Eden began.

He told them that the whole story began to make sense after Shele Ocevan was killed.

"This much I know. There is a cult, sect—whatever you want to call it—operating out of Rainelle; it got started in the 1800s and it's still around. I'm not sure how deeply the cult was involved in the murders, or if the members even knew about them."

They accidentally injured or perhaps killed a young girl who was participating in one of their rites or ceremonies. Afraid of being discovered, they consulted with some of the cult's higher-ups who decided to cover up the accident so they could keep the group from being revealed.

"I don't know if the Rainelle members even knew how the cover-up would be accomplished," Eden said. "Aside from their calling for help, I've never been able to get a handle on how much local involvement there actually was.

"I'm pretty sure the guy that confessed—Joey Dulaney— killed one or more of the girls but I'm also sure Myra Kinchloe—and maybe one other—was killed by someone else involved in the cover-up.

That's what messed everything up. Joey confessed to all

four killings—to sort of enhance his insanity plea—so Buckey shut the investigation down. With no real evidence, there wasn't much else he could have done at the time."

"What about Amara McClure's death—suicide?" Dave inquired.

"I'm convinced she was killed by Shele Ocevan," Eden stated emphatically, as if it were a fact. "And, I'll tell you why. If you remember, Amara was found locked inside her house, no way someone could get in to shoot her—right?"

Eden told them he found a way into the house through an abandoned coal chute that led through a coal bin and into the house. "Shele swore she had never been in the basement and didn't know the house could be entered that way. I knew that was a lie because, later, I found coal dust on her second pair of shoes so, I know for a fact she had been in that coal bin."

He said he thought Shele entered the house and shot Amara McClure with Amara's own gun as she lay napping in her bed. She secured the house and left just before the neighbors and police arrived to discover the body.

"Why on earth did she kill that poor woman?" asked Alna.

"Probably figured she knew too much and, after all, she was secretly a cult member and she was working with the Sheriff's office. They were afraid she might rat them out—who knows?"

"That leaves us with Shele Ocevan, who do you think killed her?" asked Dave.

"I think Shele was killed when a pickup truck pushed her and her car into the path of one of those coal trains you always see around these parts. It's pretty ironic because she had a real phobia about being killed by a train. To answer your question Dave, I don't know. My best guess is that it was Aingeal Farrell or one of the other elders or someone who is still out there—still amongst us—probably a Rigdonite. It's very likely the same person, or persons who may be trying to kill me."

"I don't get it, began Alna. "Okay, why in the name of

sanity did Shele Ocevan and Aingeal Farrell agree to help you and Buckey on the case? Makes no sense to me at all."

Eden expressed the same feeling because he had pondered on it for months after Shele was killed. The only scenario he could come up with was that initially Shele wanted to get into the investigation to muddy up the waters and divert the investigators from any clues or evidence they might gather. She was also to report her findings back the superiors of the group.

"Why not kill you like everyone else? Hell, by this time one more wouldn't have made much difference; why keep the charade going? You think they were playing cat and mouse with you?" said Alna.

"You never know, but I like to think she had a thing for me. Believe me, I have every reason to accept that idea. I mean aside from an ego thing. I think she just wanted to stick around. And, I really believe in my heart, that—more than anything else—is what got her killed."

"But why in the pluperfect hell involve Aingeal? It was pretty much a done deal when she came onto the scene, wasn't it?" Dave asked.

"Again, no way to know for sure, but I suspect she was brought in by the elders to check to see that everything was smoothed out, to see if there was anything, or anyone else that needed taken care of. I figure she bugged Shele into letting her meet me."

"One last question," began Dave, "given all of your suspicions, why didn't you just turn over what you knew to Buckey."

"I wonder that myself sometimes. I think now I should have trusted him; hindsight is a wonderful commodity. It was an election year and many of the folks who vote in this county may be involved in this mess. I'm not sure if any of them actually had anything to do with the killings—anyone alive at least.

"You have to understand, I simply don't have any hard evidence. Since that time, someone burned the cult's meeting place and the whole congregation has either disbanded or gone underground. To me all of it is plausible, but who knows where it might have gone. I know Judge Canfield would never touch it—I don't think any judge in his right mind would.

"I don't have to tell you about the policing authority of Pennsylvania sheriffs, let alone their deputies. It's a pretty muddy area, so the State Police and even the locals look upon a deputy sheriff who might interfere in a case they solved, might see the deputy as something of an upstart.

"Alna, I know you must be confused. When I get some time, I'll go into this in more detail. Dave is pretty much up to speed now, but you don't know as much about the details as he does."

Chapter 10

The wind swept across the lake bringing a stinging mist that, if it had been a few degrees colder, would have resulted in ice clinging to everything it met. The summer tourists were gone and the town had been buttoned up in anticipation colder months ahead. The days continued to grow shorter, but the cold made them seem to endure in a way that would last until the first spring thaw.

Caitlin Dalaigh had returned from southwestern Pennsylvania and had given her final written report to the venerated Elders of the Kivas of Fundamentalist Rigdonites. The group had all the look and feel of a group of Rotarians meeting to discuss business as usual.

James Henderson and Enrico Moratti had returned earlier to report they had taken care of what was known as "The Problem." They had taken Myra Kinchloe from the sacred Kiva of the Pennsylvania congregation and disposed of her in the nearby game lands. A single gunshot to the back of her head had been the means of covering up the actual cause of death, which had been an electrical shock. A high-voltage charge had passed through her body when she was placed on some sort of apparatus during a bizarre religious rite.

When it became apparent that Myra's roommate Elizabeth Mayow knew much more than she should have, she was eliminated by Henderson and Moratti in much the same fashion as Kinchloe, except in her case, the gunshot was not a cover-up. It was the cause of death.

In her oral report, Caitlin Dalaigh told the elders that she was known in George County as Aingeal Farrell and Orla O'Shea went by the name, Shele Ocevan. Caitlin told the elders that she had, with the help of one of the congregation, eliminated the heretic Orla O'Shea and went on to explain exactly how this had been accomplished.

Caitlin also informed the Elders that there was one existing problem in the southwestern Pennsylvania community— Deputy Eden Whitloe. The case was made to eliminate the deputy because he was the remaining person—outside the cult—who had any direct knowledge of "The Problem." Moreover Orla O'Shea (Shele Ocevan) had become his lover, and there was no telling how much she had revealed to him.

"The upshot is, we have quite a mess down there and it's much worse now than when this whole thing began," she explained. "I certainly hope you don't think I'm responsible for this slipshod, misbegotten mission."

"Oh, I don't think there is any way this casts aspersions on your abilities; no one is going to blame you." said the Illustrious Leader of the sect. "We'll discuss it and get back to you about continuing your assignment."

With that, the Elders retired to discuss the problem further in the inner sanctum of their place of worship. From the outside the form of the building looked pretty much like the one that had served a similar purpose in George County. On one end there was a circular stone structure and attached to it was a large building that enclosed what would normally be called a sanctuary. There, the similarity ends; the Pennsylvania building was crude and rough-hewn by comparison. The "Kiva" (The circular silo-like part.) was polished granite and where the sanctuary in Pennsylvania was board and batten, the sanctuary here was stainless steel, glass and tile.

"Do you think Jim and Rico can handle this without it becoming a total debacle?" asked Delwyn Brody, the leader of the group of six elders. "I don't want this to go any further, it's messed up enough as it is."

A whispered discussion followed with some of the Elders angrily arguing different positions. A spokesman for the group raised his hand and was recognized.

"We don't see why it should take two people to go down there to take care of one deputy sheriff," said the spokesman.

"Oh, he's The Sheriff now… but I'm afraid you misunderstand. I didn't mean for Jim and Rico to take care of that issue. I'm asking if they can be depended on to take out Miss Dalaigh."

The group chorused, "Oh."

The spokesman began, "That's different, I don't think any of us would object to them in that circumstance."

"We may not need a tallied vote on this and I surely don't want a recorded vote. Is anyone opposed?"

"I'm not opposed, just a question," said one of the younger men. "Doesn't the elimination of some members run counter to Rigdon principles?"

"Oh it's the essence of the teachings of our glorified leader Doctor Rigdon. When the body—the tree of the Church—is threatened it is the duty of the elders to take action even if that means cutting off a rotted limb. I think that's almost a verbatim quote from The Book. You see, a defective limb can drain the essence of the trunk, the body, an essence that is necessary for the survival of the tree. There being no opposition, James and Enrico are hereby assigned the task of removing Miss Dalaigh from the membership rolls—permanently," said Brody.

"Now to the main issue before us."

A discussion of who would take care of Sheriff Eden Whitloe ensued.

"I'll have to look over the situation and the membership down that way. I'm not sure if any of the current members have the skills or the stomach for it, but given enough incentive, I'm sure we can find someone who is up to the task.

That whole congregation down there seems to be in disarray and in need of a bit of discipline. If it were up to me, I would eliminate the whole membership. You know they burned down their own Kiva and for all intents and purposes suspended operations. All this after we, at great risk to our movement, covered up their mistakes for them? They claimed an outsider burned the place, but I never believed that for an instant."

* * * *

At the first meeting with the new sheriff's staff Dave seemed to get on well enough. Since he was older, none of them seemed inclined to test him with sophomoric practical jokes or fool's errand assignments. He had the unique ability to become best buddies with everyone in sight, even the people who ran the place—the janitor, the maintenance man and the receptionist. Alna insisted on not being introduced and preferred to stay in the background. Given her experience and relative youth this was perhaps best. Eyebrows were sure to be raised when folks learned she was working with the sheriff.

Eden's main concern was for their safety. He was reasonably sure that Dave could take care of himself, but he worried about Alna's abilities when it came to firearms. He feared that someday all of their weapon's training might be put to the test.

At an informal meeting in his office he brought up the subject of self-defense. Alna and Dave looked at each other knowingly and smiled. Eden noticed Dave's attempt to stifle a bemused grin.

"Okay, what's so amusing?" he said.

"Let me see your weapon," Alna replied.

Eden hesitated at first, but then pulled out his automatic pistol, ejected the magazine, cleared the chamber, and handed it to her without returning the slide to operating position. The first thing she did was check to make sure the chamber was clear, next in less time than it takes to tell, she slipped the slide catch and allowed the chamber to close, then completely field-stripped the piece, laying each part of the weapon in military order on his desk blotter.

"Very impressive," Eden said. "Now let's see you reassemble it."

"Oh, I don't put 'em back together, I just know how to take them apart. You'll have to show me how you do that part."

Dave, who knew she was kidding, handed Alna his scarf. She placed the scarf over her eyes and held it in place while Dave tied it tightly in position.

It seemed as if it was one of those speeded up movie scenes. Alna quickly found each part, as it was needed, then assembled the firearm, in seconds, as if it were something she did every day before breakfast.

So as not to appear too intimidated, Eden said, "If I had known you were going to put it back together that quickly, I'd have had you clean and oil it while it was apart."

Alna returned a forced smirk.

"I suppose we can forego the firearms training session," said the obviously impressed Eden. "Bet you can't hit the broadside of a barn though."

A trip to the shooting range would prove that both Dave and Alna were superior to anyone on the staff—including the two Slaughter Bubbas—when it came to marksmanship. Their skills at handling handguns and long guns were considerable and unquestionable. Eden would also learn Alna wasn't quite up to taking on anyone twice her size, but she was no slouch at hand-to-hand combat either.

Chapter 11

A funeral director is a necessity in every community and fortunately for Rainelle, Andrew Walbridge was around to perform the service in George County. He knew he would have trouble being accepted into Rainelle society even if he joined the Presbyterian Church that was directly across the street from the courthouse and he also knew he would encounter trouble in any attempt to meet the girl of his dreams. Most folks were polite enough, but most folks don't really want a constant reminder of their mortality around either. He could sense it even in his best friend, Randy Winter. He suspected Randy thought he was sizing him up for a casket and burial vault — which was true. It was a professional thing with Andy. He always had trouble with the ladies, was considered effeminate and not much of a catch. Running around with Randy didn't help either. Andy was far from gay — although he had secretly considered necrophilia more than once — folks stared referring to their friendship as that Andy-Randy thing.

They met when Walbridge applied for a business loan and they sort of hit it off. Winter eventually invited Andy to join his lodge. Lodge of the Runes, he had called it and Andy was convinced the organization was something like the Moose, or maybe one that was secretive and socially and fiscally helpful, like the Masons.

Eventually Andrew Walbridge found the Lodge of

the Runes was merely a front for a more sinister sect of Fundamentalist Rigdonites.

Andy Walbridge came to curse the day he got involved with the Rigdonites and he was beginning to have recriminations about getting mixed up with Randy Winter. Maybe he couldn't blame the disaster everything had turned into on Pauly Loughman, but he heard rumors that Pauly was talking with Lin Kelley just before the murder case began to unravel. He also had terrible misgivings about some other members, as well.

Andy decided to meet with Randy under the pretext of discussing Pauly's future with the lodge. His mind was nearly made up however. Pauly—one way or another—had to go. The meeting he had in mind was to feel Randy out and try to determine how much he'd blabbed to the investigators. Things were so screwed up he didn't know who to trust, where to turn, or what to do next.

Walbridge's Funeral home was experiencing hard times. The last couple of funerals had been cremations and the big bucks derived from embalming, caskets, vaults, cemetery plots and headstones, all of which helped on the positive side of the ledger, weren't forthcoming. He secretly thought of a new endeavor he would brand as "Burnemnflushem", but someone had already beaten him to it. Additionally, none of the elderly were cooperating. They were moving out to Florida and Arizona and didn't return home for the traditional Walbridge treatment in the numbers Andy was expecting. When they did return, it was more often in the form of ashes in a cheap cardboard box. You would think, among the ones that were left, a few of them would be considerate enough to die at home so that he could at least make a decent living.

The Andy/Randy meeting was held in one of the empty funeral home viewing rooms where there would be no interruption, unless one of the more responsible elderly unexpectedly happened to help make Andy more solvent. Not a likely event at all, from what Andy concluded after a recent hospital check.

"What's this all about?" asked Randy.

"I really don't know. You know how messed up things have been recently and I thought we could talk it over and come up with some ideas," that's all.

"Messed up? What do you mean?" Randy asked innocently.

"Damn it, Randy, don't give me that shit and don't try to play dumb. You know what I'm getting at," Andy looked over his shoulder as if to assure himself no one could overhear. If anyone was around it was a few funeral home ghost hangers-on.

"The murders—the lodge—the Rigdonites. You're in this as deeply as I am and don't you forget it. If you do, I'll damned well be here to remind you."

"Oh."

"Yeah, Oh. You and that Aingeal Farrell—and don't try to play dumb. Everyone in town knows about her and I'm one of the ones who think you were doing her too. You know why I think so?" Andy challenged him.

"I don't kn…"

"Taste."

"What do you mean by that?" Randy asked.

"Taste—you ain't got any. I suppose when you're desperate… hell… I didn't call this meeting to talk about your taste, or lack thereof. What I'm saying is you two were pretty chummy and I'm assuming you told her a lot about the inner workings—the secrets of—our organization. Hell, you even nominated her for membership, and we both know she was initiated."

"You mean did I tell her anything about the other churches—or—uh, the elders? Is that what you're getting at?"

"You tell me."

Randy paused, then began, "I swear to you now and if

need be before the Venerated Elders, I didn't tell her any more than I would any initiate. Nothing, you got that? Nothing!" he emphasized.

For Andy's taste, he was too adamant. He knew Randy was lying, but for the sake of his inquiry, he moved on.

"Okay, I'll believe that. (When hell drips with icicles) Let's move on to Pauly Loughman. Do you know anything about what Pauly might have revealed. I know he was babbling his fool head off just before all of this stuff started to break."

"You know Pauly," Randy protested, "He gets a few drinks and wants to feel important. If I wanted to know what he's been spreading around, I'd snoop around Lin Kelley's place. She's real easy to get information out of."

Andy knew it would just make things worse if he asked around about Pauly. Nothing would pique Lin's interest more than a couple of questions about the village idiot. At that point, he decided that both Paul Loughman and Randy Winter were rotted limbs that would have to be pruned to save the tree, although he wasn't so much concerned with the tree as he was with his job. If any of this got out, his job, his life would be ruined.

He kept Randy talking for quite a while, hoping he would change his mind on the decision he had reached but his mind was made up. When the meeting had run its course, he went home and sat down to read the Georgian Observer. He started to go to the kitchen to explore the possibilities of a late night snack as he glanced in as he passed his gun cabinet. The first rifle was his favorite, the one he always used for deer hunting.

He took it out and absently opened the chamber of the 30-30 lever-action carbine and sighted through its Leupold 2.5x Scout Scope at the image of an actor on TV. Andy thought of his Red Ryder BB gun and the old movie A *Christmas Story*. I'd better not shoot someone's eye out, he admonished himself with a wry smile.

Chapter 12

Enrico Moratti, if not for living in rural New York would have been the archetypical mafia hit man. He was a walking cliché with jet-black, Vitalis-slicked hair, a dark suit and Giorgio Armani sunglasses. After meals he retained a toothpick far too long, incongruous for the countryside, but most in keeping with an image he didn't particularly want to project—a Joe Pesci bad-ass attitude.

Rico and Jimmy Henderson were everything the typical Rigdonite was not. The elders kept them around with money and they used them as "security agents" when the need arose. This isn't to say that Rico wasn't a devoted Rigdonite. He was an ex-Catholic and when he took on the new faith he did it with conviction and fervor that matched his grandmother's certainty that Catholicism was the one true faith and everyone who wasn't a Catholic was going to have a hell of a time in the hereafter.

On the other hand, James Henderson was along for the ride. Not as bright as Rico, he looked more like Irish Mafia and ten watts dimmer but he hung out with Rico and what was good enough for Rico was good enough for him. Jimmy had reddish blond hair and wore a sort of frock coat over a black turtleneck and khakis. Both men made their living in— you guessed it—the used car business. Their car inventory ranged from legitimate, through various degrees of warmth, to absolutely hot. Jimmy wasn't a genius, but he had a real knack for knocking back odometers.

"Jimmy, I know the elders assigned this thing to both of us and that's the way it's going to be, but I'll do the actual lifting if you know what I mean. You okay with that?"

"You figger I'll get in the way?" asked a disappointed Jimmy.

"Naw, you know better than that. I just think it'll make it easier all around. Two guys, two chances of getting caught, ya know?"

"Hey, if you wanna' be the one ta bust a cap on her, be my guest. I wuz never too keen on shootin' any angels anyway."

"What makes you think I'm gonna shoot her?" Rico asked.

"See, I jump to conclusions. You're right, I wouldn't be any help to you, just a hindrance."

So, it was decided that Enrico Moratti would remove Caitlin Dalaigh, a.k.a. Aingeal Farrell from the membership rolls.

* * * *

Caitlin Dalaigh wasn't born yesterday. When she gave her report at the meeting with the Venerated Elders she knew, perhaps before the members of the group, that her days with the Rigdonites were numbered. If she had been the docile figure that the sect's women were supposed to be, she might have accepted her fate. However, the words docile or pliant were words missing from her lexicon. In their place were words like determined, tenacious and for good measure, obstinate. She was determined she would not go gentle into that good night, she would rage against whoever—or whatever they sent against her. Caitlin didn't just have attitude she *was* attitude.

Andy Walbridge was right Aingeal/Caitlin was never going to get by on her looks. She had a Carrot Top head of bright orange hair, the consistency of steel wool. To her advantage in a fight, she was built more like Evander Holyfield than say,

Oscar De La Hoya. Although she had a certain appeal for some men, she looked more like Abe Lincoln, (complete with mole) more Aristotle than Jackie Onasis. Come to think of it, Randy Winter had no taste at all in women; desperation overcame aesthetics every time.

After the meeting Caitlin began thinking of where she might go. At first she dismissed returning to George County, it would be the first place they would look. On further consideration, it might be the last place they would consider because it was too obvious. She might just call up Randy to see if he was up for a Bristol Mountain skiing vacation.

Caitlin knew she was no prize either in the looks department or even Miss congeniality but she also knew that her main competition in Rainelle was the stiffs Andy Walbridge might have in his cooler, so getting him to invite her on a whim wasn't completely out of the realm of possibility.

"Hello," said a voice on the other end of the line. "This is Randy Winter."

"Hi Randy," she said ebulliently. "How ya doin'? It's Aingeal."

"Aingeal?"

"Hey Randy, it's me. How many Aingeals ya know?" she said with just the right degree of anger in her voice.

Winter was dumbfounded. He assumed when Aingeal left, right after Joey Dulaney confessed to the murders, he'd seen the last of Aingeal Farrell. She had told him it was her final goodbye, dumped him and headed for the door—never to return, so to speak. At least that was his perception of what had happened. (He didn't know it, but that was exactly her intention at the time.) He was disappointed that she just up and left him, but was also relieved to have her out of his life. Foolishly he assumed everything would eventually get back to normal after Joey confessed to the crimes.

"Hi Aingeal, what's up? I didn't think I'd ever hear from you again after that long goodbye. I had that dumped feeling, if you know what I mean?"

"Aw, Randy, you know how it is. Things change, things happen. I thought I'd go back home and… I miss you. Don't you miss me? I thought we were good together."

Chapter 13

Cameron West Virginia is midway between Moundsville and Littleton, which is to say the middle of nowhere, USA. With a population of a little more than a thousand, its heyday had come and gone. Oil and gas, then some glass manufacturing and a pottery came and went. It was the same story as several of West Virginia's middle of nowhere places.

Joey Dulaney walked the streets of Cameron, West Virginia for a couple of hours while he tried to decide his next move. He wasn't penniless, but darned close. On a quiet side street he managed to jimmy the moneybox of a newspaper vending machine and found himself sixteen dollars and fifty cents richer. It wasn't much, but it gave him some breathing room for a while.

A street marker indicated he was on Mountaincrest Boulevard, as he turned left onto Highland Avenue, he hurriedly walked down to a side street that was deserted. No reason to hurry, he strolled along in the evening dusk looking for a mark—a car that looked ripe for the pickings. There was little chance he would find something that met his idea of an easy set of wheels, but he needed some sort of vehicle. What he found was definitely not a cool means of conveyance by any stretch.

He scrounged in a worn pocket and found the remains of his favorite candy, a Gazebo bar, a commodity was nearly impossible to find. When intact, it had all the appearance of the Baby Ruth Bill Murray had found in the pool in a memorable scene from the movie, *Caddyshack*. Baby Ruths and Joey's Gazebo, when it was intact, had the look and texture of, well—a turd. He made a mental note to buy a box of Gazebos as soon as he made his first big score.

Hope Heflin was sitting on a sawn off stump that had been a row of elms that once lined what was once a more upscale street. She was seventeen and had about every rebellious trait a teenager could possess. Her face was filled with acne and belligerence that her nose ring did nothing but enhance. She was the sort that one might expect to assume the trappings of Goth, but no spiked hair for her and no pale-faced makeup. Hope was a little over five feet tall and although a bit pudgy, of average weight. She had a rounded face that some might find cute, but most would be hard-pressed to call beautiful. She had the look of an Ozzie Osborne daughter about her. To set off the persona she was lamely trying to project, she had a Marlboro hanging loosely from her lips a habit she considered cool and very, very adult.

"Hey, boy! What you doin' with my mama's car?"

Hope nor Joey had any way of knowing it was a line straight out of Arthur Penn's Bonnie and Clyde—vintage 1967.

"Whatcha' mean?"

"Your tryin' ta steal it, ain'tcha? Ain't you ashamed of yourself?"

"I was thinking about buying one just like this," Joey said defensively.

"If you had any money, and I don't think you do, what would you want with an old shitbox like that anyway?" Hope challenged as she flipped the remainder of her smoked butt at his feet.

"I got enough money for some soda pop. You want to go down town and find a place where we can get some?" It was an attempt to deflect the accusation and to get to know his newfound friend a little better. Lord knows he could use a friend.

"You must not be from around here, there ain't much of a downtown if you want to call it that. There's a little place down there we could go, if I don't get stuck with the tab for the pop."

"Come on downtown with me now, we can talk," he offered. "What you doin out here in the street, you some kinda orphan?"

"None of your business."

"Bet you're waiting on your boyfriend to come and pick you up."

Hope ignored his suggestion. "What kind of work are you in—when you ain't stealin' cars?

"I don't have a job right now, but I'm looking."

"I bet you never had a job. You look like a homeless drifter to me."

"I just got out of the prison, up in Pennsylvania, he said hoping to shock her.

"What was you in for, stealing little old ladies' handbags?"

"Murder, I'm a serial killer," he said, hoping for a shock effect that would stop her in her tracks.

"Sure you are, I know when somebody's messin' with me, you ain't no serial killer, unless you were causing little old ladies to have heart attacks when you robbed 'em."

Joey smiled, she returned the smile as he reached out his hand and said, "Let's go get that pop."

Hope Heflin took Joey's hand and they walked off into the darkening evening.

The diner was just that and little more. They served some food, but Joey wasn't going to waste the little money he had by buying a meal for Hope. He ordered a bottle of Pepsi for her, which arrived in a can, and a bottle of root beer for himself, which arrived in a bottle.

"How about some straws, or a glass for the lady?" Joey

challenged the counter boy.

The geek behind the counter looked at Hope and gave her a knowing wink. "Sure," he said, "anything for her highness. Coming right up."

They passed the early evening with small talk about how Hope was doing in school. It seems she went to school when she felt like it and most of the time she didn't feel like it. Her step-dad didn't like her attitude, of which she had plenty. Her recently deceased mother just suffered her adolescent defiance as a "phase she was going through." Hope's adolescent phase had probably hurried her mother along to an early grave.

"I know I'm different from all the other kids a school. I know I got something they don't. Not sure what it is yet, but I know I'm not like the rest of them hicks. You know what I'm sayin'?"

"Yeah, I think I do," said Joey, shining her on. "I could see that right off. You ain't like any other girl I ever met before. You're—like—special. I bet someday you'll be a celebrity just like in the magazines and on TV."

"Well, it ain't gonna happen if I stay around here. Ain't nobody gonna discover me in Cameron, West Virginia."

Joey noticed it was getting quite dark and he knew he might have to walk back to his cabin, so he suggested he walk her home. He also suggested she find him some food when they got there.

"Tell you what, I'll fix you a sandwich and put some stuff in a paper bag. I'll slip out the side door and hand it to you if you wait out here. I'd invite you in, but it would be a hassle that neither one of us need"

With that she disappeared into the house for what seemed like a very long time. Soon she appeared at the side door with a bag. She handed him the bag and asked, "Be honest, you was gonna steal the Chevy when we first met, weren't you? How you gonna get home—if you gotta home that is?"

"I'm good a hitchin'. I just stand out there with a miserable hang-dog look and someone will come along..."

She interrupted with an upheld finger. From the finger hung a set of keys. Joey looked at the keys and smiled. She returned his smile and said, "Make it easy on yourself."

He reached for the keys as she snatched them back, "Not so fast, you ain't getting these until we have an understanding. If you take that car over there, you're gonna take me with you. That's the deal, one package, the car and me."

"I don't mind hauling you along, you can even stay at my place for a while, but there's something you gotta know up front."

"Yeah, I know. All you guys want the same thing. I don't mind..."

"Well, I ain't gonna be your lover-boy..." Joey began.

Hope attempted to protest that having a lover was the furthest thing from her mind, but he continued.

"It ain't that I'm gay or anything like that. I just ain't wired that way. I like you well enough, but when it comes to doing that, I'm not up for it, if you know what I mean."

"I know...," she began.

"No you don't. I don't mean I can't get up for it. It's just that *I don't want to*—that's all."

"Oh."

Joey had no way of telling her that the deep exciting thrill that he always sought only came when he consummated the encounter by killing his partner. He knew she didn't believe he was a killer, and he wanted her to continue her delusion. He wouldn't admit to being crazy or anything like that. The only explanation he could come up with for his weirdness was that he wasn't wired like other people, not crazy—just different. He was different and no one could understand how he felt. He knew the only way to avoid killing women was not to be intimate with them.

So, Hope Heflin got into a 1983 Chevy Malibu with a ticking time bomb, on her way to a future that didn't include being discovered for stardom.

Chapter 14

It was a lazy Sunday afternoon and an early arrival of winter was in the air. No more squirrels, no more rabbits, no more turkeys, only a few deer hiding in the tall brown grass alongside the road waiting for a chance to trip the light fantastic in front of an oncoming automobile. The sky was a shade of murky purple suggesting a change in the weather—perhaps snow.

Sheriff Whitloe had no real reason to call on his new deputy, he was just seeking out someone to talk with, someone he could trust. Dave seemed not all that surprised to see him.

"What brings you out on a day off, you workin' overtime? Come to think of it, how much does the county pay for overtime?" Dave asked with a grin that suggested he knew the answer to the overtime question already.

"Yeah, that'll be the day. You ask for overtime pay from the taxpayers in this county, they'll bitch about it for months," Eden returned the grin.

"Been finishing up some projects I started before I assumed the duties of deputy. I'm not moonlighting, just catching up. Hope you don't mind."

Except for a slight shrug, Eden didn't respond.

"I don't know quite how to put this," Dave began, "but I've been thinking...

"Go ahead, just let 'er rip, always ready to hear some of your thoughts."

"It's been a few weeks now and we haven't turned up much on Buckey's murder…"

"Look Dave, we ain't gonna turn up much. We'll be damned lucky if we ever learn anything more. I've often wondered why some more kill-for-thrill creeps don't shoot up the countryside more often than they do. They go out there, set up a little sniper's nest, take out someone on a highway, then run like hell. If they're careful, don't leave shell casings or cigarette butts no one would ever catch them. About the only way to get a lead on a person like that is if they talk, go to a bar, get drunk and spill their guts. If they work alone and keep their mouth shut, chances are they'd never make a ripple. Look at the Unabomber—you know, Ted Kaczynski—they would never have caught him if his brother hadn't turned him in."

"I'm thinkin' the same thing, but you know, that feller is still out there somewhere. He's spooked right now because he took down the wrong man, but he'll be back. A person who would lie in wait and shoot somebody the way he did is determined. That's what worries me."

"Shit, you're worried?" exclaimed Eden, "What do you think I do most of the time? I check the hillsides when I'm going to work, I listen for noises around the place at night and wait for someone to just stroll into my office and shoot me. I may be fatalistic about the whole thing, but there's not much else I can do," Eden said.

"Brings me back to my original point. You got an extra room out there on the creek, a sofa or place to sleep?"

"Oh no. You ain't movin' in with me. Get that notion out of your head."

"Hey, don't get upset with me, I just thought you could use some company for a few days. Two guys are a hell of a lot harder to take down than one."

"You know what they say about fish and company. We'd probably be at each other's throats in no time. I can see it now, Sheriff Felix and Deputy Oscar, me the neat freak and you the slob. A fine odd couple we'd make."

"What makes you think I'm a slob? My place is neat enough, thank you very much," Dave tried his best to sound insulted.

"Old hippie fart, bet you haven't taken a bath since Woodstock," Eden joked.

Dave could see there was no convincing Eden, so he simply put it as directly as he knew how. "I'm going to come over to your place for an overnight stay. You can throw me out if you want to, but I'll put the word out all over town you're an inhospitable jerk—and—and—I'll tell Lin Kelley on you. You're gonna have to run for election before long you know. She'll be tellin' everybody you're a real asshole. And—and, I'll check the perimeter every evening and every morning before you even get your lazy butt out of bed."

The discussion/argument was interrupted by a phone call from Dan Brackenridge.

"Hello," answered Eden.

"It's Dan, Dan Brackenridge down at the state police barracks."

"What's up Dan? You got something on the guy that's taking pot shots at me?"

"Maybe. I just got word that Joey Dulaney walked out of the joint about five weeks ago."

"What? Just up and walked away?"

"That's pretty much it. Dressed up like one of the visitors and went along with them out the gate and down the road. Look now, don't get your bowels all in an uproar. I don't think he'll head this way because he knows it's the first place we'll look. I figure he's headed over into Ohio, or up to New York. He has to know the heat is on down this way."

"Thanks for the heads up Dan. I think you're right about him putting distance between himself and George County, but the news doesn't make me rest any easier. I don't think he would have any interest in me anyway. If you remember, he wanted me to negotiate a plea for him. We parted on fairly friendly terms after he copped on the whole deal."

"Yeah, I know, but it never passed the smell test for me. I know the little bastard is a nut-bar. You take care now, ya hear?"

The next day Dave moved into the guest room on Random Creek and eventually—like Sarge the cat—he became just another minor annoyance in Eden's routine. He would have to admit that Dave was company and he made the ride to work more pleasant. Of course Eden never admitted to anything and he kept up the pretense of being aggravated by Dave's presence.

Eden usually watched the evening national news and sat down, remote in hand, and readied himself for the daily assault to his sensibilities.

"Why you have to watch that Fox News shit? You some kind of reactionary?"

"Just what I'd expect from an old fart hippie. You flower-power girls just couldn't wait until you got another war to protest could you?" Eden said to goad him on.

"I bet you listen to Rush Limbaugh on the office radio," Dave came back at him.

The banter was interrupted by a backfire from a vehicle on the road in front of the house. The loud report sent both men scurrying for their side arms that they left on a small living room table.

They looked at each other, broke into a grin and laughed. If they had seen the car and its driver, they might have been less ebullient. If they had looked out the window, they would have seen a 1983 Chevrolet Malibu station wagon speeding off to the west.

* * * *

"Just what the hell was that all about?" asked Hope. "You'd just love to get somebody on your ass wouldn't you? I'll bet the law's got a bulletin out for you."

"I told you, I'm a serial killer, I'm wanted throughout the

entire tri-state region. I'm a dangerous, murderous badass so don't be givin' me no shit," Joey warned her. He'd heard some women like the bad boys, so he decided to lay it on thick. Hope slid across the seat and snuggled close to him. "Ya know, I'm starting to believe you are one bad mutha." She brushed his hair out of his eyes, slipped her hand under his arm and pulled it close to her.

He shook himself free. "You better get back over there before you start something I'll have to finish," he told her.

"I think I'm more than you can handle, you get started and I'll finish you off."

Joey didn't reply and just stared out the windshield at the flakes of snow driving toward them.

"We gotta do something for money soon," Hope began. "I'm not going to lay around that shack all day with no TV and we're gonna need to get gas for this thing before long. It had a full tank when we got it, but that was four days ago.

"I'd knock over a gas station up on Route 250, but I don't want to draw attention over here. There's no way they'd think it was me, but if someone sees me...

"I think I can get some money," Hope began again.

"Where you going to get money, go home and rob your piggy bank?"

"You sure you're not the jealous type? You know what you said..."

"Look, you're last thing I'm interested in that way. You're free to do whatever floats your boat," Joey interrupted.

"Just checking. There's a man who lives about seven miles below Cameron, an old geezer who must be at least fifty, name of Lonnie Loftstead. Anyway we met at a football game and he gave me a ride home once and things sort of developed from there."

"I don't believe it! Little old Hope Heflin, a geezer squeezer. Who'd a thunk it? Don't tell me, let me guess, you let him do you?"

"Thought you weren't the jealous type? Back off, we were just friends. Of course I let him believe he had a chance and we fooled around a little. He was like a big hound dog sniffin' after me."

"You think this Lonnie will give you some money if you was to ask him real nice?"

"You never know. I'll give it a shot. I may have to be real nice to get very much outta him though. You care how nice I hafta be?" she asked, hoping to get him to reveal that he cared for her to some degree.

"Nope, you can screw him to death and take everything he's got for all I care."

"Turn around and head south."

"Huh?" Joey as lost in a reverie of images of Lonnie the geezer and the somewhat less than virginal Hope Heflin clasped in a hot sweaty embrace. Hope's interruption brought him back and he began to wonder how sweaty one could be when it was snowing outside.

"I'll drop you off and you can take it from there. I'll go back up to the diner and hang out. How long you think you'll need?"

Hope told him to pick her up in one hour and fifteen minutes. This caused him to wonder what the fifteen minutes were for, but he didn't ask because he was afraid she might tell him.

"If the porch light isn't on, I'll turn it on when I'm ready to be picked up. If it's already on, I'll turn it off."

A little over an hour after the drop off, Joey left Cameron and headed south to pick up Hope. She was standing on the darkened porch, stamping her feet in the cold, waiting for his return.

As soon as the car braked to a halt, she ran for the door, got in and tossed a billfold to Joey as she settled into the passenger's seat.

"Get this piece of shit moving," she said, "floor it."

"What tha hell—whatcha do, rob him? Hey you little twit, there's blood on this thing."

Chapter 15

The Blue Bird Motel and Diner wasn't exactly what Caitlin Dalaigh a.k.a. Aingeal Farrell had in mind for a luxurious winter vacation retreat. In fact a vacation was the farthest thought from her mind.

It was still early in the season and things were just getting underway in the Finger Lakes region. A cold snap cooperated and snow machines, looking much like geysers in Yellow Stone were blowing white powder into the air. Its slushy consistency accumulated on groomed trails where, like ants or raisins on icing, skiers down hilled the slopes and cross-countried well-marked pathways.

Inside, the newly painted walls and recently stained carpets, the Blue Bird provided a homey ambiance of a rest home fallen on hard times. The smell of cheap weekend whiskey, urine, turpentine and pine scent deodorant filled the tiny rooms that were heated by through-the-wall electric heat. Cheap reproduction paintings, motel furniture and plastic condom-like coverings over plastic cups waited to greet the newly arrived couple.

Randolph Winter registered while Aingeal waited in the car he had parked out of sight at the side of the building. Using the name Mr. and Mrs. Arthur Collingwood and cash, rather than a credit card, Randy attempted to cover any trace of their visit. The desk clerk didn't ask for a license number or any other form of identification because she knew most of the lodgers would rather their visit remain anonymous and unrecorded. She was pleased to offer this service in lieu of payments she would have to send to taxing entities.

Ever the gentleman, Randy carried their overnight luggage into the room and helped Aingeal settle in. While she freshened herself in the bathroom in preparation of an evening of dining, he stretched out on the queen-size bed to watch the evening news.

At Aingeal's suggestion, they called room service and dined in. The person who delivered the food left it on a cart at the door, knocked and left without checking to see if anyone arrived to take it into the room. The meal consisted of something that was, if not for the menu, indistinguishable from deep-fried sawdust balls. The desert was a scoop of vanilla ice cream with a dark brown substance poured over it. Aside from some weather-related small talk, not much was said over the meal.

After Randy put all of the room service equipment and dishes back in the cart and put it back into the hallway to be picked up, he returned to find Aingeal in her negligee, lounging on the bed.

"Okay, what's all this all about?" he asked.

"Wha... Oh, I was about to ask what was all of what about, but I know what you mean. I was having a fit of early winter depression and thought would be nice if we could get together. I know it wouldn't be the same, but maybe we could have a semblance of old times."

"Why me?"

"Oh, Randy, you know you're the only one that ever did it for me. I never had anyone like you before—or since. It's that simple. Now get over here you big dork."

Big dork? thought Randy. What the hell does she think this is this a TV sitcom scene? His opportunities for meeting someone of the opposite sex in a motel room, someone willing, were limited so he figured, what the hell.

After it was over, that's the way Caitlin Dalaigh thought of it, getting it over with, Randy rolled over and began to snore. Caitlin turned off the overhead light and now the only illumination was a glowing clock and a nightlight from the bathroom. She waited for nearly half an hour before she went to the nightstand and returned to the bed. Randy murmured as she sat down on the bed beside him.

She took the pillow from her side of the bed and arranged it on the other side of Randy's head. Next she opened the clutch bag she had taken from the nightstand and retrieved a small, snub-nose .38 caliber pistol from it. She placed the silencer-extended barrel within inches of Randy Winter's temple and eased the hammer back. Randy gave a quiet grunt one last time as the cylinder clicked into position.

Chapter 16

Caitlin Dalaigh a.k.a. Aingeal Farrell hurriedly gathered her clothing and toiletries and tossed them in her overnight bag along with a recently fired .38 caliber snub-nose revolver. She got a towel and wiped everything down she might have touched. She looked in the hall for the room service cart, but it had been taken away earlier. With any luck, the dishes and flatware would be washed and any traces of her prints would be down the drain. So far as she could determine, any link between her and the dead man in the Blue Bird motel bed had been erased. No small town investigator would use any of those CSI big city techniques of fiber collection or other esoteric evidence on this one. It would be a "hooker shoots john" scenario on any police blotter, not worth any further real investigation. She would drive Randy's car to the closest big city, catch a bus and be back home before anyone discovered her handiwork.

* * * *

The thud of a .38 behind a silencer, covered with a blanket wasn't loud wake the couple next door—even if they had been sleeping. The blonde on top stopped for a moment and said, "What was that?"

The guy on the bottom only moaned before she continued and quickly forgot she heard anything.

Outside where Rico and Jimmy were parked, there was no sound at all. "We gonna sit our here all night, freezin' our asses off?" Jimmy complained.

"I got a feeling she's gonna' come out of that place before long and get in the car leaving that guy behind," said Rico. "You got no patience. See why I wanted to be the one to do this thing?"

"You figure she's gonna dump 'em?"

"Just watch," Rico said as Caitlin slipped out of a side door, found Randy's car and opened it with his keys. She threw her bag in the passenger's seat, slid into the driver side and backed out of the parking lot onto the highway. She had no reason to look in the rearview mirror, no reason to suspect she was being followed.

She did have a reason to glance down at the gas gauge that was glowing red, with the low fuel alarm ready to go off. Not wanting to be stranded in the middle of nowhere, she began to scan the highway looking for a filling station. She passed three of them that were closed before her hopes were raised by the prospect of an intersection ahead.

Other than a lone attendant who was watching a late night or early morning television show, the station was deserted. Light from a flickering sodium vapor light cast a sulfurous glow that enveloped the gas pumps and surrounding area.

Caitlin was relieved to find the pumps were self-serve as she slipped her card into the slot in the device. She made her selections and began to pump gas into the tank without giving much notice to a car that pulled into the bay opposite her. She continued pumping, then returned the nozzle and began to recap the tank when she heard a voice behind her.

"Make a peep and you are a dead woman," said the voice.

"I recognize that voice, that you Rico? You sorry bastard."

She turned around and faced him. He was standing looking at her, no gun, just a smile and the tip of an imaginary hat.

"You know you scared the shit out of me. What the hell are you doing out here?"

Rico kept smiling as he took a .22 long barrel revolver

from his deep coat pocket and pointed it in her direction.

"Been looking for you," he said. "Get your ass back in the car—the passenger side. I'll do the driving. You make one move I don't tell you to make and I'll toast you right here. You got that?"

Caitlin's reply was to open the passenger's side door and sit down, awaiting his further instructions. Without a word, Rico got in, started the engine and turned around to head back to the Blue Bird. He pulled over and waited for Jimmy to take up the rear.

Rico pulled into the same place the car had been only minutes ago and turned to Caitlin. "We're going back into your motel room, you got the key?"

"Don't have a key, it's one of those credit card things. I... I threw it away."

"Bull shit! Now get it out and give it to me NOW."

"I think it's in my pocket or purse."

He pulled out the .22 and pointed it in her direction. "Don't make any fast moves. Get it out and hand it to me."

She reached into her coat pocket where she knew she had put the card and handed it to Rico. By this time Jimmy was standing outside the car waiting. She knew her only option was to go along with them and see what developed. Maybe something would develop and she would have a chance.

Rico took her by the arm and led her to the motel hallway through a side door that accepted the card. "Now, which room?"

Caitlin hesitated for a moment, trying to think what to do next, but Rico applied pressure to her arm. "Don't screw with me, the room number, now!"

"One oh one," she said.

What they found inside was a surprise to no one, except the two men were amazed by the lack of blood. It had been absorbed by the pillow and was all on one side of it.

"So that's the famous Randy Winter," said Jimmy. "Looks

89

to me liked you ruined a beautiful friendship," he said to Caitlin.

"I'm gonna ask this once, don't mess around, or I'll just do you right now. Where's the piece you done him with?"

"In my bag in the car," she replied quickly.

"Jimmy, go get it, bag and all. Make sure nothings laying around in their car."

Rico told her to lie down on the other side of the bed. At first she protested saying she was afraid she would get blood on her clothes, but she was persuaded by the .22 and a hopeless feeling that anything she might do now would be useless. A few bloodstains on her clothing wouldn't matter much at this point.

When Jimmy returned, he found the .38 in the bag and checked to see if it was loaded. He found one empty chamber and one chamber that had been fired recently. There were three remaining bullets in the five-shot Featherlite and the silencer was still attached.

Rico put his hand over Caitlin's mouth and held her down as he nodded to Jimmy.

Chapter 17

Rainelle, Pennsylvania is the county seat of George County and the home of Sheriff Eden Whitloe's office. The office used to be in the courthouse, but since the remodeling, it was now less than a hundred feet away. Rainelle looked like a Norman Rockwell, a painting that was done in the 1940s right before WWII. The courthouse, complete with pseudo gaslights in front looked more Thomas Kinkade—the lights providing a warm, schmaltzy Kinkade glow. Goya or Bosch could not have painted a scene that better depicted the Rainelle that Eden knew.

"Local Man: Murder-Suicide" read the headline in the Georgian Observer. "Couple found dead in motel," was the sub-head. Eden read further down the page to learn that the man was "A Rainelle businessman," who, according to coroner's report, had died first. Apparently his "companion" Caitlin Dalaigh had shot him and sometime later turned the gun on herself. Both had been killed by a single gunshot wound to the head. "No reason to suspect the involvement of others," read a drop-quote. The gun had been registered in her name.

Randy's picture was one that had been dug out of the files and there was no photograph of Caitlin Dalaigh. If it had been just about anyone else, Eden wouldn't have suspected the involvement of cult members, but he knew Randy was a member and he suspected Caitlin Dalaigh was a New York connection, perhaps she was even Aingeal Farrell herself.

The Deputy thanked his lucky stars the murder, suicide or whatever it was had taken place in another county—another state. It was something local law enforcement might have an interest in, but there would be little or no responsibility for investigating it. The Observer assigned Shelley Braun to cover the story; the assignment editor sent her up to New York to see what she could dig up. Eden knew Shelley fairly well and she could be relied upon to share whatever she found.

Shelley came back with a story that added nothing to what was already known. However she also came back with gruesome morgue photos of the motel pair she had conned some attendant into swiping for her. Eden wasn't a bit surprised to find that the picture of Caitlin Dalaigh stretched out for autopsy was the woman he knew as Aingeal Farrell.

Later Shelley sent him a rough draft of the story she had prepared for the Observer.

Hi Eden,

Please don't share this with anyone else and destroy it after you're done with it. I'm not sure what the ethics are, but I know the paper wouldn't be thrilled if they were to find out I'm sharing this with you.

> LOCAL BANKER DIES IN ALLEGED SUICIDE PACT
> CANANDAIGUA N.Y.—The body of local businessman Randolph Winter was found in a motel near the skiing resort of Bristol Mountain with a single gunshot wound to the head. According to Canandaigua authorities, Winter was believed to have been shot by a companion who later shot herself.
>
> Winter and his companion, Caitlin Dalaigh a.k.a. Aingeal Farrell, were found in the Blue

Bird Motel early Tuesday morning. Initial reports indicate Winter's death preceded Dalaigh's by at least an hour, leading to speculation about the incident.

An anonymous source revealed that in the case of a subsequent suicide it's unusual for the second person to wait for a period of time before ending their own life. However, when questioned about the time delay, Police Chief Kenneth Powers said, "It's not all that unusual a circumstance. She may have just waited for a while—could have even gone out for breakfast—thought it over, then came back and—you know— who knows what goes through someone's head at a time like that?"

At a later news conference, Chief Powers was asked if there would be an inquest or a further investigation of the deaths. He indicated there could be, but it seemed to him to be a typical case of murder-suicide or even a double suicide and there was no evidence to the contrary. He added that there was no real evidence to suggest it wasn't a double suicide.

Randolph Winter was CEO of Farmer's Bank of George County and left a... blah, blah, Blah.

Eden, I think we can put this one away. The word around the campfire up there is some other or others could have stumbled onto the scene of Randy's murder and subsequently killed Aingeal/Caitlin. I don't have to tell you that's pretty thin—pure speculation in my view.

Be sure to shred this mutha and be sure to let me know what you can do for me sometime.

Shelley

Eden read the letter over a couple of times, made a note or two and fed it into the shredder. He smiled a knowing smile as he saw the "... let me know what you can do for me sometime." slip into the shredder. He knew full well what Shelley Braun had in mind.

With Buckey, Randy and Aingeal dead and with Joey Dulaney on the loose, Eden gave up hope of anything in Rainelle or George County returning to anything near normal. For Eden, "normal" for the past several months had been nothing less than chaos and confusion. Arresting drunks from behind the Palace ticket booth and rounding up stolen bicycles were distant Norman Rockwell dreams of Rainelle's good old days. Hopefully Mrs. Welchner or Dave Bruester would come by with a complaint about vandalism or Rainelle perversion that would relieve his funk.

Chapter 18

A cold rain washed red, yellow and dingy brown leaves down the drive and into the gutter below. A Beamer sat in the driveway where Eden expected to see Dave's old truck. Was this Alna's car or someone come for him, or was this thought another of the paranoia variety that had come to haunt him?

Through the kitchen window he could see the familiar form of Alna Byrne working to prepare an evening meal in anticipation of his return. Although he was expecting to see his constant houseguest, Dave Quinn, he was pleasantly surprised to find Alna in his place.

"This is a surprise," said Eden as he walked into the living room and unbuckled his utility belt in preparation for a relaxing evening. "Where's Dave?"

"Said he had business over in Moundville and wouldn't be back until late," she replied. "Told me to come over and cover while he was gone. I didn't walk the perimeter the way he does, but I did take a quick peek outside. You can watch the evening news while I finish making dinner."

"Watcha makin'?"

"Lasagna, garlic toast and salad. You got a problem with that?"

"So Dave thinks I can't survive out here without him now is that it? Sent you out to baby sit?"

"I'm not a mind reader, but I sort of think he had two things in mind. One was to sort of keep you company while he's away and the other—well, you figure it out," she said suggestively.

"You decided to offer yourself up for it, huh?"

"I agreed to come out here and help out, if that's what you mean. I volunteered to cook, you have to do the dishes after," she said.

"Lasagna, huh?"

"And garlic toast," she replied and smiled. "Salad."

"Croutons?"

"I can cut up some of the toast if you like."

"Sounds great to me. Anything but the stuff Dave fixes. He thinks he's doing me a favor and I never complain, but he can't cook for shit. In fact that's what most of his stuff tastes like— shit. And don't you go telling him that. He tries hard to please, so I eat it to keep from hurting his feelings, but I'd just as soon pick up something from Mickey Dees."

Winter thunder accompanied the evening meal as the salad was eaten with little comment.

"Get your I.D. taken care of? Picture, prints, card?" inquired Eden.

"I thought I'd get a deputy's badge, all bright and shiny like on TV."

"Hey," said Eden in his best Frito Bandito accent, "You don't need no steenking badges."

"I thought I'd at least get the rank of deputy. It says on my card I'm a 'Special Sheriff's Agent.' That the best you can do?"

"That's the best Judge Canfield could do. He said if I made you deputy, it would have to be full time and there would be a shit storm from the County Commissioners about it. This way, you get 1099s for the IRS and you slip in under the radar. According to the judge, it's the best we can do.

By this time the meal was over and Alna was proving her threat to have Eden do the dishes was an idle one. He took advantage of the view as the attractive blonde worked at the sink. His eyes traveling down her form from her long-sleeve sweatshirt to the tight fitting jeans where they lingered for a moment before moving back up to the ringlets of blonde hair dangling above her shoulders.

Not wanting to be caught looking (leering?) he went to the living room, took a seat on the sofa and began reading the morning paper. He was thinking more about the effect Alna Byrne was having on him than about the newspaper and he became intensely aware the electricity in the air wasn't from the lightning.

"Done with the Sports Page?" she asked as she took a seat, too close, beside him; too close for Eden who was the other end of the sofa. Without comment, he handed her a section of paper then put his nose back into the habitat of Hagar the Horrible.

"You sleeping over tonight," Eden asked, trying to sound nonchalant.

"Depends when Dave gets back. Looks like he's going to be late though. I can curl up on the sofa if I have to. Don't want to have to open you up to charges of an employer taking advantage now do we?" she quipped.

"Certainly wouldn't want to do that. I'll get you a blanket and you can settle in whenever you like. I'm going to hit the hay so I can get an early start in the morning. You and Dave have anything planned for tomorrow?"

"We'll see what the morrow brings."

It must have been somewhere around 3:00 in the morning and the Special agent was sound asleep when she was awakened by an unearthly yell.

Chapter 19

Alna Byrne, fully clothed, sat up erect and alert reaching for her service pistol. She pulled back the slide to chamber a round as she eased toward the Sheriff's bedroom, finger on the safety. From inside another scream, only this time it was less a bloodcurdling yell and more a scream of agony followed by a moan.

She quietly eased over and flipped the switch on a nightstand lamp. In the middle of the bed was the figure of a man with both hands to his head who was moaning much more softly now.

Gun still at the ready, Alna said, "What is it Eden? Did someone get in here?"

He looked around and said, "No, and put that damned thing away unless you can shoot demons. I was having a nightmare—no, make that night terror. Did you ever wake up in the middle of the night, terrified beyond all reason?"

"You scared the living shit out of me."

"I'm sorry, it's something that's been happening more often lately. I'm glad you're here. I usually have to get up and walk or read or something to get my mind off of it."

"Off of what, Eden. Tell me about it," she said, sitting on the edge of the bed." She reached out and put her hand on his.

"Not much to analyze," he said. "It's really simple enough for anyone to figure out. It's like one of those '50s Sci-Fi things. Everyone in town—even the cops, the clergy, your best friend is one of them. They're all, all of them, after me. They all want to kill me or make me one of them. It's not very scary to talk about in the cool light of day and when you think about it rationally, it's pretty silly—but."

"But what Eden,"

"For a while it seems nothing will ever be normal, you feel like you are losing you mind."

"I think we all have," said Alna assuringly. With that she positioned herself beside him so that they were lying side-by-side, propped up with pillows as if in a chaise lounge.

"Sorry I scared you, but if you think you were scared, you should see it from inside here," he said, pointing to his temple.

As Alna moved closer to him, he felt none of the typical nervousness he experienced in the presence of other women, most recently Shele Ocevan. Shele had made him feel somehow inadequate or perhaps it was his own subtle recognition that she was using him—that she wasn't for him. He had convinced himself at the time it was her extreme beauty that made him feel that way, but as he learned more about Shele and her motives, the more he became more comfortable with himself. Given that Alna was attractive, he began to doubt once again. For whatever reason, sheriff or not, he was attracted to Alna Byrne.

He moved closer to her and touched her hip. She moved away and said, "Not tonight boss, maybe another time. Tonight I'm on duty and I want to be up to speed if anything bad goes down. Besides, I don't want to be caught with my pants down if Dave makes an unexpected appearance."

"I see your point." Eden said, pulling the covers over his head and rolling over to try to sleep. Alna still unnerved by Eden's nightmare slipped out of the bedroom and took up her place on the sofa and falling asleep with her service pistol in her hand.

* * * *

It was daybreak when Dave returned to Random Creek to

find Alna waiting for him at the door.

"I thought I heard someone poking around out here," she said, "I should have known it would be you."

"Yeah, it's me. I just got back from checking around the place. Now you can put that thing away," he said referring to the cocked pistol that was pointed at his mid-section. He gently put his finger on the barrel and directed it toward the wall.

"Alna, have you noticed a blue, older model, Chevy Malibu station wagon in your trips around the county?" Dave asked.

Chapter 20

"I wanta' ask you something," began Joey Dulaney. "Am I getting' sick of hanging around this dump?" Hope asked as if she had a premonition. "If that's what you're gonna' ask, you got it in spades. I've about had it up to here," complained Hope. "About all we ever do is go riding around in that beat up Chevy and burn gas money we could be using to get our asses out of this state."

"Look, I don't know what you did to that—that Loftstead fella—and I'm not so sure I want to know. I heard a rumor that a guy down near Cameron was killed by a home invader that stole his wallet—"

"Careful where you're goin' with that honey bunch. You said you aren't sure you want to know. It might not set very well for a desperado like yourself to be hangin' with an armed robber and murderer to boot, now would it? Is murderer right? Or, should it be murderess. It ain't actress anymore; they call 'em all actors now—men and women together.

"Yeah, I snuffed him. Now you got cops on your ass for whatever penny ante shit you pulled—you got accessory to murder now to boot. I figure they've tied the missing car, the missing teenager and Lonnie the geezer with a slit throat all together by now. I figure they're looking for Hope Heflin right this minute and they don't really give a big shit about Joey what's-his-name."

Joey took her by both shoulders and locked his eyes on

hers. "Lookit, you might have offed an old man as a lark, that don't make you anything like me. Not even close. They're after me for killing a couple of girls—no women—older than you. And that's the ones they know about. They figure I'm as crazy as a bed bug and by now, I'm not so sure they ain't exactly right.

"So it looks like we're in this together, just Natural Born Killers, you and me. You see that movie?"

"What movie?" asked Hope.

"*Natural Born Killers*. It was about this guy who picks up a girl and they go on a killing spree. I never saw it, but I heard about it."

"You mean like Caril Fugate and Charlie Starkweather?" Hope asked innocently.

"Who?"

"Ancient history, back in the '50s—James Dean and all that good-old-days crap. I read about 'em in some fan magazine. They's just like you and me—or them natural born killers you was talking about," Hope explained. "Only Ole Charlie and Caril were the real deal, not some made up bull shit. They made a bunch of movies about them too. Springsteen even wrote a song…"

"Don't go trying to talk me into some sort of Caril and Charlie scene. I'm not the sharpest when it comes to this stuff, but I know they fried ole Charlie and Caril found Jesus and is, or was, dyin' of old age in Michigan," Joey broke in.

"Okay boy genius, let me explain it to you this way—" Hope explained that they were both on the run from murder and were beyond any chance of redemption. If they were caught, the very best they could hope for was to spend most of their remaining lives in prison or some mental institution.

"I ain't got no worries about the death penalty. First they don't execute young girls but better yet, there ain't no death penalty in West Virginia. For all their hick/boob image, their justice system don't kill people. On the other hand, you—

you're screwed. They catch you, you're goin' right to the death chamber, if you're lucky. Or you could spend the rest of your days in a seven by ten rubber room with a bunk and steel toilet. Maybe have your own bubba-lover for a cellmate. That what you want?"

Joey didn't quite know how to reply, "Whatcha got in mind?"

"I don't know about you, but whatever happens ain't gonna turnout good. I've been watching TV and looking at magazines all my life; seems to me anyone who stands out in this world gets to be famous one way or another. John Kennedy, for everyone in West Virginia that loved him, wouldn't amounted to a hill of beans if he hadn't been shot. Everyone remembers that Kliebold guy and his what's-his-name buddy that did the high school killings."

She evidently missed the irony that she didn't remember Eric Harris's name.

"I don't know about you, but I'm gonna go out taking some folks out with me. When I go, I want to go in a big splash—no not a splash, a flash—like one of them shooting stars. Do something that folks will remember long after I'm gone."

Joey had to admit, her argument had some appeal. He knew he would eventually be caught and if they didn't execute him, he'd spend the rest of his life in a nut house or prison. He wasn't quite sure about checking out though. He was sure he didn't want it to hurt—maybe a quick gunshot to the head, or getting blown away in a suicide bomb, would be painless.

"So, whatcha got in mind?" he said.

Chapter 21

"Damned if I can figure this one out," proclaimed Dave as he walked into the sheriff's office, head bent, looking over some papers he was carrying.

"What's that you got there Dave?"

"It's the final autopsy report, back from the state. How long's Buckey been dead now—weeks?"

"Hey Dave, you live and work in a bureaucracy now, I got to explain that one to you?"

There was a short pause as Dave read the report. About halfway down the page, he stopped. "Nothing much until you get to this part here," he pointed to the paper. "Says here he had early stages of adenocarcinoma. Ain't that some kinda cancer?"

"Let me see that," said Eden. "Yeah, it's some sort of pancreatic sarcoma. Hmm, Buckey said he wasn't feeling well and went to see a doctor a few days before he was killed.. I'll have to check that appointment out and see exactly what was up with him. I don't think it will change anything though."

"You know some folks get news like that, they look for a quick way out—pancreas stuff is one of the most deadly. Not too many recoveries from that one," offered Dave.

"Now Dave, there's no way Buckey could have committed suicide…" Eden began.

"No way unless he had help. I know it's pretty farfetched, but we got only a few theories. One, he was shot by accident.

Two he was shot by someone who wanted to kill him—or you. Three, he was shot by someone he convinced to—well—you know."

"Assisted suicide? You gotta be kidding me. Who would be that loyal and that dumb? Ah—hold the thought—let me think that one over. Who would do such a thing for money? This is George County for God's sake. It's overpopulated with mental giants who would kill their mommy for money."

There was a long pause that Dave let just hang in the air.

"You thought about it yet?"

"I'm thinking, I'm thinking," complained an irritated Eden. "In the meantime I'm thinking of who would just up and kill Buckey. He or she wouldn't have to know about his cancer, you know."

Because Buckey had no enemies and was almost universally loved, only a couple of really good murder suspects readily came to mind. Kathy Robinson or Bill Robinson.

I'm really reaching. Could the Kathy Robinson thing have gone further than he suspected? It was hard to imagine Oliver Buckey as a backdoor Lothario—a philanderer. Naw, too Peyton Place, too soap opera-ish, not even worth mentioning. Still and all, Eden knew he'd hit a nerve when he kidded Buckey about taking Kathy out to the state park.

At that point Eden made a mental note to call Kathy Robinson and squeeze her just a little to see what might pop out. If he learned nothing there, he'd take a cut a good old hubby Bill.

* * * *

Kathy Robinson was decent enough looking in a housewifey sort of way. She was probably hitting her late forties or early fifties, about the right age to start playing around, Eden thought. When she came to the office, she was as nervous as Nun in a nudist camp. She was dressed in a housewife frock and wore a housewife cardigan over what must be a fairly well preserved figure. *Hard to tell what's under there.* Her hair had a touch of gray that gave her a sophisticated church lady look, not severe, just conservative looking.

"What's all this about, Eden?" she asked in a quiet, gentle voice that broke slightly.

"Just checking with some of the folks that knew Buckey. Strictly for the record—so I can say I conducted an enquiry—I suppose people will say," the sheriff said with a knowing smile.

"You did know him pretty well, didn't you?"

He intended for the know to come out as know in the Biblical sense but he made every effort to avoid a lecherous tone or anything to connote the double entendre he intended.

"Sure did," she said almost enthusiastically. "Bill and I sat next to him in church every Sunday and had him out to our place for dinner several times a year. We really miss that sweet man."

Right about here, Eden began to have his first doubts about the idea of a Buckey/Kathy affair. No matter how hard he tried, he just couldn't picture them in bed together and when a picture almost formed, he immediately banished it from his mind. It was sort of like picturing your mom and dad doing it on a Saturday morning while you watched cartoons.

Knowing Bill Robinson for the quiet, pious family man he was and knowing Buckey for the man he was, Eden decided to forego questioning him. Maybe there was a chance he was wrong about the Robinsons, but this line of investigation seemed like a dead end. Moreover, there was no one else to suspect as a killer, so the avenue of assisted suicide would have to be pursued.

* * * *

Eden gave the task of inventorying the sheriff's office arms. He was busily checking the assigned side arms against a list he had on a clipboard. Everything checked out perfectly until he began checking the list against the guns in the storage locker.

"Eden, you know you've got a .45 caliber Thompson back there?

"Tommy gun? Yeah, someone picked that up as war surplus after WWII. Civilians need a special permit to own a submachine gun, so there wasn't much demand for it back then. It's a collector's item now, maybe we should look into selling it."

"Only thing that seems to be missing is a .30-30 Marlin Lever Action."

"That thing's an antique too, real popular back in the '50s. Hey isn't that what Dr. Vinnie said he thought might have been used to kill Buckey?"

"I think you're right."

"Be a hell of a coincidence. We got a missing .30-30 and Buckey was killed by one," Eden commented.

"Don't go running off into la-la land. Vinnie said he thought it might be a .30-30. It's worth doing a diligent search for the weapon, but I doubt if we turn up a murder weapon. Who knows when the last inventory was done, who knows if it was overlooked then. It could have been missing for decades.

Eden, Dave, Alna and Arleigh along with the janitor and maintenance man searched the office from top to bottom; they even looked in the ceilings and the drains in the rest rooms. There was no sign of the gun.

Eden thought back to when he and Dave were discussing the possibilities of assisted suicide. Who would be that loyal and that dumb? Only one name came to mind— Arleigh Slaughter.

Chapter 22

Delwyn Brody called a meeting of the elders to discuss how they might deal with the "problem" in southwestern Pennsylvania. He had thought long and hard about who might be assigned the task of eliminating the remaining person who was likely to know something about the situation there— Sheriff Eden Whitloe.

"This is an informational meeting, but I want your advice on how to proceed. I have a couple of names of people who might be able to accomplish the task at hand. I won't reveal their names to you because it might put you in jeopardy as accessories. You are better off not knowing."

The Illustrious Venerated Elder told them he would send Brothers James Henderson and Enrico Moratti down later to assure the matter was closed. If the need arose, he would send them earlier to assure the person would, in fact, complete the "task."

"It appears to me they are a pretty gutless bunch down there, and the person I have selected may need some encouragement, if you know what I mean," Brody said as he concluded the meeting.

* * * *

If no one had known the Rigdonites, they would have never expected them to have a hunting cabin in a remote part of Washington County. For the owner, it was a weekend get-away more than a hunting retreat.

It might have come as a surprise when a cell phone rang, but being near the Interstate, the signal was loud and clear.

"Hello"

"Do you know who this is?"

"Reverend?"

"That's all you need to say. Don't say anything else, unless I ask a question, understand?"

"Yes."

"Good. I have an assignment for you."

Brody continued to convey the assignment to the cabin owner. He also cautioned that if they didn't feel up to the job, to let him know now. Once undertaken, the assignment was not evadable and compliance would be enforced with "extreme prejudice."

"I would be extremely disappointed if you avoid the assignment—if you get my meaning. Please indicate your assent with a simple Okay."

"Okay."

The connection ended.

* * * *

Not far away, but far removed from the, if not posh, comfortably furnished hunting cabin/getaway, was a cabin of another sort. Outside the shack, hidden in a brushy cove and covered by a light snow sat a Chevy Malibu. Inside Hope Heflin and Joey Dulaney argued and planned for their future— what little of it remained.

"So you want to go out like a shooting star? Be just like—I was gonna say— a serial killer. They ain't that many female serial killers."

"Aileen Wuornos," replied Hope.

"Who?"

"The woman Charlize Theron played in the movie *Monster*.

"I suppose you could call her that, but there still ain't that many."

"I'll start a trend. No, there are lots of couple-killers, you stick with me, we'll snuff a bunch of squares, get famous and go out in a blaze of glory. If we're real careful, we might get away for years. Hell, Bonnie and Clyde lasted four years," Hope argued.

"Yeah, but they was more robbers than killers. They say Bonnie never killed nobody. Besides, they didn't have a lot of hi-tech stuff to catch them with back then."

"Who gives a shit? Give me knife or a gun and I'll show you what a natural born killer is."

"Who you gonna start with. Let's get this show on the road," Joey said with more bravado than he felt.

"I'd do my momma first. She'd be number one on my list, but she's dead. Hepatitis beat me to it, so I'll have to start with number two, the asshole she married. He was husband number four for her, turnin' tricks doesn't do a whole lot for a stable, loving relationship I suppose. Anyway, my step-daddy, the ever lovin' pervert is at the top of my list. I'll leave it up to you to figure out why. You don't have use much imagination. I suppose he thought he was some kind of great lover, but his abuse was physical and mental."

Hope explained how she would like to sneak into his house at night and how she really liked the feel of the knife when she cut Lonnie Loftstead. She told him guns were too impersonal.

"Might try to do him real slow. Cut him bad, but not right away fatal, let him bleed out slow."

Joey felt a shiver up his spine. *Hell, I think I found someone crazier than I am.*

Chapter 23

Arleigh Slaughter, now there's a thought. He had access to what could be the murder weapon. Hell, he could have had it for months—years even. He was out at that end of the county when Buckey was shot. He was a relative, maybe he would inherit Buckey's pitiful estate and maybe there's an insurance policy.

Eden had been going over the assisted suicide possibility, arguing back and forth inside his head for hours. The most convincing thing about the argument that Arleigh was involved and that it was suicide was the relief that could come from knowing that he wasn't the intended target. He could send Dave back to making furniture and Alna—well, he might have her stay a while to sort of wrap things up.

He went outside where a light snow was falling into a dark afternoon, breathed in the sharp, cold air and thought— *to be free at last—no death sentence hanging over his head.* Unfortunately there would have to be a confrontation with Arleigh, but that might be the easy part.

Arleigh, like Buckey lived alone. Arleigh always thought living a bachelor's life was a normal state of affairs for a dedicated lawman. After all, he reasoned, lawmen are like undertakers, not many women want to spend much time with someone in a deadly or risky business.

He had just come in from feeding his hunting dogs, a chore he particularly enjoyed. He didn't leave them tied out as did many of the county's hunters were wont to do. Sometimes he brought one of his doggy friends in to provide some companionship for a lonely evening. As it turned out he was glad this wasn't such an evening.

Arleigh expected the caller to be one of his relatives stopping by to chew the evening's fat, but was surprised to see the new sheriff knocking at his door. He opened the door to find a shivering lawman standing on his porch.

"Hi ya Eden, this is a surprise. What brings you out on a night like this? Kinda chilly out there on the porch, come on in."

"Hi yourself. There are some things I need to talk with you about, Arleigh, that's all. Some things I need to get cleared up," Eden explained.

"Hey, if it's about some of the time I've been taking off, I've got a real good excuse—"

"That's not it, not it at all, Arleigh. Can I come in and could we sit down for a talk?"

Arleigh wore bib overalls, a plaid shirt and work boots with the rawhide laces untied. He wore a military style buzz cut; he had always fancied himself as a sort of paramilitary type. This evening, he looked for all the world like the stereotypical rural primitive, white trash bachelor and he had the political philosophy part down to a "T." Although he would have been hard-pressed to identify with Republicans, he was a Ronald Regan—not neocon—but Conservative with a capital "C." He made right-wing nuts seem sane. Right to life, anti-gun control, anti-gay marriage, God and Country, law and order freakazoid. To Arleigh, the Second Amendment was the law of the land and the Constitution didn't need to go any further than the right to bear arms part.

He invited Eden to take a seat at a kitchen table while, although unasked, he poured coffee for both of them.

"So what's up?" Slaughter asked as if he didn't have a clue.

Eden thought it best if he proceeded like he already knew more than he did—and as if he had some evidence to back it up.

"You have that .30-30 Marlin around here somewheres, Arleigh?" he asked.

"What do you mean? You think I took the damned..."

"Now don't play around with me Arleigh," Eden interrupted, "I have someone at the office that says they know you took it."

"Someone? What someone, who?"

"I'm not going to play that game with you, Arleigh. I know you took it and I also know you used it to shoot Buckey," Eden said with as much determination as he could muster, which was a whole lot more than he felt.

"What the... you think I stoled that rifle and you think I shot Sheriff Buckey? Eden, are you out of your ever-lovin mind?"

Eden couldn't think of anything else to say to add weight to his accusation. "I know what I know, that's all. Whatcha got to say for yourself?"

To Eden's surprise a sudden change came over Arleigh. He'd never seen him look so determined. There was a lengthy and awkward pause.

"Lookit, Eden, I been around this business since you was throwin' footballs in high school and makin' goo-goo eyes at little cheerleaders. You may think I'm not the bullet with the biggest bang, but I'm not as dumb as you think I am either.

"You don't have any idea where that gun is and if you was going to arrest me, you'd have the cuffs on me by now. You ain't got diddley squat. I know it, you know it, so you might as well admit it right now. Even if I did kill Buckey, I'd' a been doing him a big favor. You know that."

At this point Eden tried to interrupt, but Arleigh was on a roll.

"And don't go givin' me a bunch of that left-wing socio-blubber about whoever killed him did wrong—and, you and me, let's just leave God out of this, Okay? I ain't saying I did it, but I got myself convinced it wasn't the wrong thing to do." As an afterthought he added, "Whoever it was that did it."

Eden was less self-assured when he asked, "Did you do it Arleigh?"

"Tell you what, Eden, everyone has one of those places where they forget things. A place they put things away and they're never, ever spoken of again. Let's you and me put this back there and go on from here. You know you got a loyal deputy you can depend on, you don't need one you have to be lookin' over your shoulder thinking you don't have someone you can trust. Eden, if you ever need me at your back, I'll be there. You don't have to look around for me, you know I'll be there for you. If you can leave it like that, I can."

The sheriff really had no other choice. He had played out his bluffed hand and Arleigh had called him. Without the confession he was hoping for, he was in a position most lawmen have to deal with.

He knew Arleigh was guilty—Eden had never mentioned mercy killing to him, but he seemed familiar with Buckey's "need." Just like the Pretty Maiden's murders, he had to live with something he knew but couldn't prove. Arleigh knew and Eden knew there wasn't one shred of evidence. Eden suspected the rifle was dismantled and maybe even melted down by now. At least now he knew the person that killed Buckey wasn't after him and he felt the freedom of a man who had a death sentence lifted.

Chapter 24

Boy this is stupid, thought Joey Dulaney as he sat just off Highland Avenue in Cameron, West Virginia. The loping idle of the Malibu didn't do much to steady Joey's nerves during the wait. A steady snow was falling, hopefully disguising the car a little. He felt every eye in Cameron was on the recently stolen Chevy.

Boy am I dumb, he thought as he considered the fact Hope Heflin had talked him into this whole thing. She said he would only get in the way and ruin her plan. He was to wait in the car while she took care of her stepfather Homer Heflin. It would only be about fifteen minutes she promised, but according to the car's clock, it had been thirty — and counting.

Nearly an hour had gone by and Joey was considering putting the car in drive and heading out without her when Hope came running down the street toward him, she slid to a stop in front of the car and fell, stumbling full-tilt into it. She made it around to the passenger's side and fumbled with the door handle.

"Stomp it Honey Bunch," yelled Hope who looked like she'd been fighting with a Tasmanian devil. Her hair and clothing disheveled, bespattered with blood and speaking in short breathless sentences, she managed to tell him she had been delayed because she was looking for money.

"I did get a couple of thousand, wanted it to look like a home invasion robbery. Would you believe it, he had some

115

bimbo in there with him? She was on crutches too so she didn't cause much of a problem. That's about his style, pickin' up some cripple. Now I got two notches—no, with Lonnie, that's three, it's your turn, Killer Babe. Who you gonna' do first, that deputy fella you was talkin' about?"

Unfortunately, Joey told her his plan included the use of a rifle and he had no use for a knife in his "line of work."

"Wish you'd'a told me that when we was back yonder," she said thumbing in the direction from which they came. "Head on back that way and I know where I can pick you up a rifle gun."

"Bull shit, we ain't going back there. It's gotta be crawling with cops by now."

"It's only been dark for a few hours. Nobody's going to find those folks until morning. You drive back and I'll run in and snatch that rifle. I know right where it is and if you don't have the nerve to go back, I'll know what you're made of."

Reluctantly, an even more nervous Joey headed the Chevy back to Cameron. Once again, he parked at the head of Highland Avenue and waited for Hope's return.

When she got back to the car she was carrying a gun case. She opened the door and pushed the case into the back seat.

"Good thing I went back, his girlfriend was still squirmin' and moaning to beat hell. I had to get a butcher knife out of the kitchen and stick her again. Pretty big mess back there," she said as she settled into the seat.

"They're gonna' really be after us big time now for sure," Joey complained.

"You want to go do the deputy now? I got shells for the gun and everything. I think you should get him done while we're on a roll. You wait too long, you'll lose your nerve," I know that about you lover boy, she said teasingly.

Joey didn't want to tell her he had already lost his nerve so he told her to get in and shut up. They were going back to their hideout cabin and lay low for a while to see how things developed.

"We'll check the radio in the morning and see if they are looking for us. If they are, we might have to make a run for it over through Ohio. Maybe even try for Mexico—shit—I don't know."

"We ain't going nowhere until you get that deputy. That's what you said you was gonna do and now you got to live up to your word. If you don't kill somebody now we ain't together on this. You gotta do it or we ain't a team—you got that?"

Joey complained that they had driven by Eden's place several times and had found it guarded. The couple he had working with him walked a perimeter and guarded the house closely. He told her it would be best to wait a while until things cooled off a little.

"Yeah, we wait and you're the one that cools off. You lose your nerve," Hope replied. "You got the balls for this, we go right now, over to Ohio and rob a gas station or convenient store and you kill the clerk, honey. That's the only way we can be a real-deal killer couple."

So it was that Joey Dulaney and Hope Heflin crossed the Ohio River and made their way in their Chevy Malibu to Powhatan Point, Ohio. It was late evening when they stopped at Tommy's Carry Out store. Except for an unfortunate Emily Weaver, the clerk for the evening, the store was deserted. Emily was filling in for Tommy who was attending the wedding of a close friend.

With Hope in the driver's seat, Joey fiddled with the old Marlin carbine until he finally got some shells into it and jacked one it the chamber.

"Just like old Chuck Conners—*The Rifleman*," Joey remarked, wishing he had a more compact pistol.

He clumsily tried to hide the rifle by holding it at his side and down his right leg. And screwed up his courage while Hope egged him on.

As soon as he entered the place the usually less than

observant Emily screamed when she saw Joey juggling the carbine. She immediately hit a key on the cash register, grabbed a handful of cash and threw it toward him.

"Here, take it," she shouted, "take it all. Don't hurt me. You don't have to hurt me, I don't know you and I won't tell anyone."

What was going on in Joey's head at this point was anyone's guess. To him it seemed he was somewhere else and someone unknown to him was standing in Tommy's store pointing a gun at an extremely frightened Emily Weaver. Emily was totally freaked out and screaming like a banshee. The noise unnerved Joey who was frightened out of his wits and utterly confused.

"I ain't even supposed to be here tonight," she wept.

Wherever Joey was and whoever was holding the gun, it fired with a report that filled the room. To anyone nearby, it must have seemed to fill all of Powhatan Point.

Emily would never say another word. The bullet entered her throat and she collapsed choking, living long enough and making sounds to haunt Joey's nightmares for the rest of his short life. Joey scooped a few bills from the floor, nearly dropping the rifle. He turned and hesitated for just an instant, went back to the counter and grabbed a box of Gazebo bars and ran for the door and the waiting Malibu.

Once inside the car he began to feel sick as adrenalin drained from his body.

"Don't get sick in the damned car," cautioned Hope. "I ain't gonna' clean it up and I sure as hell ain't cleanin' you up."

Chapter 25

Snow continued to pile up for the rest of the day to the point that Eden was considering giving up and calling to tell the receptionist he was taking the day off. He had spent a restless night trying to think how he could get Dave off the case since he was no longer under a death threat. He couldn't tell him, oh by the way, Arleigh hit his intended target, Sheriff Oliver Buckey. He wasn't looking for me. You see, Buckey made a deal with him—. Shit, he was stuck with Dave for a while longer.

So, he would continue his "investigation" as if nothing new had happened. The idea of an excuse to investigate the Rigdonites wasn't unappealing to him—if any Rigdonites were left, that is.

* * * *

Lin Kelley's saloon wasn't known for the sign that hung over the entrance, "THE WAGON WHEEL." Everyone called it Lin's Place. There was nothing distinct about it and that's what made it so distinctive. From the buzzing neon Iron City sign in the window to the constantly playing TV in the corner, the smell of stale beer and faint whiffs of urine from the rear made it like every other working class bar. Eden remembered a line from Proust, "When nothing else subsists from the past, after the people are dead, after the things are broken and scattered—the smell and taste of things remain poised a long time..."

"There was a couple of strangers in here that night," said Lin Kelley in response to Eden's questioning. "Hey, if I'm gonna be working for the new sheriff, don't I get a badge?

"You don't need no steenking..."

"Yeah, I heard that before. Don't know why you think it's funny. Don't worry; I don't want one. You'd lose your best source of information and I'd lose all my best customers."

"Now what about the strangers, Lin?"

Since Pauly Loughman had been found dead in his car, Eden was worried about foul play. It appeared—or was made to appear—that the drunken Loughman had passed out or had fallen asleep at the wheel and took and unintended left turn off of Koontown Hill Road and his car wound up upside down in the middle of Hooter's Run.

Hooter's run wasn't deep enough to drown Pauly, but the three hundred foot drop did a number on him nevertheless. The car was found with Pauly spread into the roof liner like chunky peanut butter.

"One of them was an American, just like you and me. The other was sort of dark and oily, like an Eye-talian or Spanish feller. Maybe Messican," Lin continued. "Joe Bill Tusten claims he was talkin' with 'em for a while—tryin' to mooch drinks from them I figger. Says they were from up north—New York state maybe."

That got Eden's attention. Pauly was known to hang out with Randolph Winter and the late Andy Walbridge. He was the one who blabbed about a secret cult, opening the local Lodge of the Runes up to scrutiny. Now he was dead and there were two guys nearby from upstate New York— Rigdonite territory—the evening Pauly was killed. It was all too convenient for coincidence, "but..." There was that "but" again—no proof, just circumstantial coincidence.

"Anyone else around, or was it just Pauly, Joe Bill and the two strangers?"

"There mighta been a couple in the back booth, I don't

know if they left before Pauly came in or not," Lin replied.
"The two guys, did they leave before or after Pauly left?"
"They left right after Pauly did. They seemed in a hurry
and I thought they mighta been hurrying to catch up with him."

* * * *

"Yeah, we checked all that out," Dan Brackenridge
confirmed Eden's suspicions. "I know what you're thinking,
Eden. You never give up do you? You got it figured that
everyone who gets killed in George County is the victim
of some conspiracy. You want to think all county deaths
are somehow connected to the murders that Joey Dulaney
admitted to doing.

"You don't get off'a this thing, Eden, you're going to
make yourself sick. You hear me? Pauly Loughman was a
drunk and he didn't need any help getting himself killed. He's
no different than any of the other drunks that have a few too
many, then run off a steep cliff somewhere. Lord knows there's
enough steep cliffs around here to oblige them."

"I suppose you're right," the sheriff began.

"You know I'm right, think about it. Take a few days off,
get some rest, take a date to a movie. Think about something
else for a while. Get yourself back down to earth and you'll
see things more clearly.

"But Dan," Eden began again.

"I know, you think there is someone after your ass and I'll
have to take the blame for putting that idea into your head. It's
been weeks now and if anyone was going to try anything, they
surely would have tried by now. You can't live under a rock."

"I've gotten over that one. Don't feel guilty for putting
it in my head either. I'm pretty sure now no one is out there
gunning for me and I'm sleeping a lot better these days."

"Don't get to feeling too comfortable," Dan began, "I just
got a report from over in West Virginia that Cameron's had two
home invasion robberies. Somebody killed a guy who lived
alone—slit his throat—and another man and his cousin were

butchered. Looks like some kind of sicko who enjoys robbing and then killing folks for no reason. The couple who were cut up—his teenage stepdaughter is missing. They'll probably find her raped and dumped somewhere."

Chapter 26

In an early winter warm spell turned the snow that had fallen turned into gray slush along with Eden Whitloe's mood. He really wasn't up to welcoming visitors but when the call came from Alna Byrne, he was willing to change his mind, if not his mood.

"Hello," said Eden in an emotionless tone.

"Hello yourself," replied Alna. "Whatcha' up to out there in the sticks?"

"Well it ain't Upper St. Clair, but it's warm and homey. You want proof, come on down."

"You know, I was about to ask for an invitation, sounds great. You get some corn to popping and I'll pick up some wine for mulling and we'll spend the evening like an old country couple."

"Well, as they say in the game shows 'Come on down!'"

"To tell the truth, I'm in Rainelle right now, so I'll drop by in about twenty minutes."

When Alna arrived, Eden took her coat and bottle of merlot (Eden hated merlot) and ushered her to the couch. He went to the kitchen and brought out bowls of popcorn and wine glasses.

"I'm a man of my word, you wanted popcorn, you got popcorn. It ain't Orville Red-n-whatzit, but it's good George County Autumn Blaze. I think you'll like it."

Alna moved closer and put her hand on his. He responded

by putting an arm around her shoulder and pulled her closer.

"Real cozy," she murmured.

"Better yet, you're off duty," he said reminding her of the last time she visited.

"Yep, no uniform, no guns, no badges."

"We don't need no steenking badges," he said responding to the opening.

"I fed you that line 'cause I know you're predictable."

"Si Senorita," he followed through, demonstrating his predictability.

Alna explained one of the reasons for her visit was to get the lowdown on the cult Eden and Dave had talked about earlier.

"You said you would fill me in later and it's been quite a while," she complained.

"Sure you wouldn't rather watch a movie? I got some good ones on the TiVo. And a couple of chick flicks too."

"You mean the chick flicks aren't all that good?"

"Like you said, I'm predictable. Here, take a couple of minutes and read this," he said, handing her five pages from a laser printer. "I'll fill the wine glasses and bring in some veggies."

Alna pulled out a pair of reading glasses and began:

* * * *

CHAPT. I.

AN EPITOME OF SOME PART OF THE AUTHOR'S LIFE & OF HIS ARRIVAL IN AMERICA.

As it is possible that in some future age this part of the Earth will be inhabited by Europeans & a history of its present inhabitants would be a valuable acquisition, I proceed to write one & deposit it in a box secured - - - - so that the ravages of time will have no effect upon it that you may know the author I will give a succinct account of his life and of the cause of his arrival which I have extracted from a manuscript which will be deposited with this history.

* * * *

"Okay, I'll bite, what the hell is this and what's it have to do with anything."

"Go ahead and read a few more pages. I want you to get the flavor of it."

Eden sipped wine and nibbled popcorn while he massaged the back of Alna's neck as she read.

"Interesting," she said upon finishing, "interesting but not thrilling. What am I supposed to be getting? What is this stuff anyway?

"That my dear Alna," he said in his best Inspector Whitloe tone is '*The Manuscript Found*' written by the famous—or if you prefer—infamous, Solomon Spaulding."

"Ah... yeah—so?"

Eden proceeded to explain that Solomon Spaulding's novel; "*Manuscript Found*" is claimed by some to be the foundation of the "*Book of Mormon*". "Some authors claim the Joseph Smith Mormon story of the finding of golden plates was made up from Spaulding's novel," he said.

"The LDS, that's the name the Mormons took, The Church of Jesus Christ of Latter-day Saints, take the position the whole thing is preposterous and heresy," he explained.

Eden told her Joseph Smith's claim is that an angel by the name of Moroni, came to him in a dream and revealed the location of buried golden plates, engraved plates that would be translated into the "*Book of Mormon*". The plates contained a story about Native Americans who Smith says were the Lost Tribes of Israel and how they were visited in Pre-Columbian times by Europeans.

"The problems with all of this are that dozens of hoaxes

were perpetrated in the 1800s and there were just about as many wild-eyed prophets running around as there were regular folks. No one knows quite what to believe when it comes to this stuff. Academic careers were devastated when their theories supporting hoaxes were exposed. Legitimate scholars are gun shy concerning just about anything that went down at that time so, to a great extent, it's tough to get any good information on anything during the period."

"I'm beginning to be sorry I asked for details," Alna complained.

"Don't worry it gets worse. In addition to the pseudo science, there were several people—wild-eyed prophets, no doubt—who knew enough about the physical world to take advantage of the numerous gullible believers."

Eden related the arrival of one Sidney Rigdon who was an associate of Joseph Smith and may be the real link between the Spaulding story and Mormonism.

"Some claim he was the real founder of the Mormon movement. Sidney Rigdon was excommunicated by the Mormons and founded his own church that was a 'Rigdonite' faction of Mormonism."

He explained that the Rigdon he and Dave suspected of being the founder of the cult that was operating in George County wasn't even a Rigdon. He was a person who took on the name, Walter Rigdon, so he could assume the authority of a founder. He let his followers assume he was related to the Rigdon that was excommunicated.

"Here's what Dave and I think happened. This false Rigdon was a radical who was caught up in church politics, he saw how Sidney Rigdon started a Mormon religion of his own, so he went about establishing his own version of a 'Lost Tribes' religion. He buried some stones—probably couldn't afford gold plates—discovered them, using the '*Manuscript Found*' story as a basis for his own cult.

"He added some stuff about South American and Pre-

Columbian Indians, mixed in some Anasazi, Adena and Hopewell legends, a liberal sprinkling of other mysticism as it occurred and there you have it—Fundamentalist Rigdonism, Walter Rigdon (or whoever) style."

"You mean folks in George County have been practicing this—this religion since—since..."

"We think as early as the 1840s," Eden finished for her.

"Okay, I think I'm getting there, but why the need for all the secrecy? What are they hiding? Why are they killing people to keep their big, bad secret?" Alna asked.

"This particular 'Rigdon,' wanted a more powerful cult-like entity. If you've studied cults you know they usually have some primal control over the followers. In the case of David Koresh, Jim Jones and even some of the fundamentalist Mormon-like cults, the ticket is sex. Think about it. What is more primal and basic?

"The induction into this particular cult is a metaphorical marriage between the initiate and a cult member who represents the membership as a whole. The marriage involves the consummation of the union that I'll leave to your imagination. It's a rite that doesn't respect gender.

"We suspect that at least one woman killed her husband after he forced her to go through the ceremony but that's a whole other story. What I don't know, or have any way of knowing, is a gnawing suspicion concerning the Pre-Columbian aspect. Aztecs, Incas... you know... they practiced human sacrifice on a grand scale. Could this be an element of Rigdon's cult? Who knows? It could go a long way toward explaining their militant enforcement of secrecy. Another aspect is plural marriage, or at least wife trading. Don't forget that some of the fundamentalists have been accused of child abuse, so there are plenty of reasons for secrecy Anyway, here's the rundown, at least so far as Dave and I have figured.

-A rift in the Mormon Church.

-Some guy names himself Walter Rigdon and sets up a cult

based on '*Manuscript Found.*'

-The cult includes elements of '*Manuscript Found*,' South American and Pre-Columbian Indians they believe to be 'Lost Tribes.'

-A veneration of the Ark of the Covenant, interest in astrology and geomancy and earth forces.

-Later some Carlos Castenada crapola and use of peyote—and, oh yeah—and some pretty bizarre initiation rites."

Eden explained that they believe the cult members are responsible for the death of at least one, or more, perhaps many more, members. From what he can determine, he believes one of the deaths came as a result of the misuse of a 19th century electrical apparatus whose purpose was to amaze and mollify the membership.

"As nearly as I can determine, Walter Rigdon built a replica of the Ark of the Covenant and put a leyden jar in it—that's a big capacitor for storing electricity. He would charge up the jar with static electricity and shock non-believers into becoming the faithful. Anyone who came into contact with it would have the bejeezzus shocked out of them—if they weren't killed."

"Oh God," exclaimed Alna, thank goodness the sect disbanded after all the killings. What's this list of names at the end of page five?"

Aingeal Farrell *
Amara McClure*
Andy Walbridge
Carl Dulaney
Harry Rishoff
Harry Woodyard
Mikail Pavlock
Pauly Loughman*
Randy Winter*
Shele Ocevan*

Ted Dunlow

"That's a list of the people I know for a certainty are members. The ones with the asterisks were members. You can begin to see belonging to the Rigdonites isn't a guarantee of longevity. Those members are dead. And, if you think the cult has disbanded and everything is okey-dokey, forget about it, the killings continue."

"And there are others still out there?" she asked.

"I figure at least that many, probably more. The big wigs of the group are located in upstate New York. That's sort of the center of who knows how many sub-groups. Locally, there are more people that I suspect are members, just because of the way they act or whom they associate with. Now can you understand what a district attorney would do with the evidence I have?"

"Brrr," said Alna as she hugged herself, "makes Upper St. Clair seem downright warm and homey. Which reminds me, I have to be getting back. Big day tomorrow."

"Since you are off-duty, I was hoping you would stay the night," Eden suggested hopefully. "I can fix you a nice place in the spare bedroom..."

Alna stayed the night and the spare bedroom stayed empty.

Chapter 27

It was an evening of an early winter snow. The flurries that accompanied Joey Dulaney and Hope Heflin to Cameron had turned into showers, then freezing rain, then sleet and finally six inches of new-fallen snow. The early morning saw the mercury dip to the teens and at that point, desperate to stay warm, Hope moved into the palette that Joey had arranged on the floor. She cuddled close to him to in hope of staying warm.

"You're my baby, you're my man. You did real good honey. Now we're a pair. Now we're bonded, together, just like being married, only better," she murmured. "We'll make them other serial killers look like small-timers compared to Hope and Joey."

Joey couldn't help but notice that Hope had given herself top billing.

Later as the newly bonded pair lay together, Joey, awakened and became aroused. For him, arousal was something to be feared—feared because for him, it was a precursor to murder.

For sleepless Hope it was a welcome sign of affection and new acceptance—a sign that also brought a dichotomy of feelings that had been awakened years earlier by step-daddy Homer. Affection, appreciation, love, passion, approval, self-esteem and raw, unbridled sex—all wired and cross-wired into her less than complex psyche. Whatever was going on inside

Hope Heflin's head, Joey Dulaney took full advantage of it that morning.

* * * *

As suddenly as the snowstorm began, a thaw followed. The storm bringing the snow was followed by a warm front that settled over the steep hills and caused fog to rise from the bottoms and hang in the valleys.

The way to the hard road was treacherous. Slushy remains of deep drifts covered the rutted pathway that passed for a country road in this part of the county. Soothed by the hum of the old gas hog engine, Joey was comfortable behind the wheel. He felt the weight of the old beast would suffice to see him through to a road that was plowed and treated with salt and cinders.

It was the first time in months that he was alone. He had friends, doctors and caretakers at the mental hospital and until last night, Hope had at least provided company enough to be a distraction from the loneliness he now felt piling up on him like the slush on his windshield.

I don't need her. I don't really need anyone now. All I need is the gun in the backseat to work with and when I'm done with it, I'll eat it like a well-deserved snack. His experience in the convenience store was a new one. He had never killed a woman in quite that way. He convinced himself this one was an accident, not meant for his usual "time" with a woman — unintentional and not ending the way his other killings had. No electrically charged thrill. Now Hope, that one was different. That one was more like it because it had feeling, he could feel it deep down in his gut, and below. He convinced himself he must be a natural born killer. If it were not so, he wouldn't have such a deep need.

A psychopathic feeling of euphoric relief replaced Joey Dulaney's initial loneliness. No longer was he concerned about being re-captured by the law. He had no fear of being killed. His only concern was that he might encounter pain in the process, but he found his new lack of concern for self was exhilarating. He was free to kill as many as he could until his string ran out. Maybe he could stay on the unidentified list like The Baseline Killer or—yes that Zodiac guy.

Joey decided whenever he killed someone, he'd leave a cross-hair drawing, like what you would see through a riflescope—just like the Zodiac guy. They might even think he was old Zodiac himself because that was one of many a serial killer who was never caught. He was driven to explore killing the way it had been with the store clerk. He thrilled at the thought of getting away with murder. Perhaps he was a cool, collected killer, like Henry Fonda in *Once Upon a Time in the West*—Frank, the natural born killer. Not crazy and frenetic like Richard Widmark, but alone, within himself, awesomely cool.

Chapter 28

The weather was typical of early winter in George County, Pennsylvania—soggy, foggy, cold—but moreover, depressing. Alna had been gone for two days, back to Upper Saint Claire to take care of her business. Except for a short-lived trip to the office, Eden kept to himself and to his bed, claiming illness—the flu he claimed. His symptoms were more of the clinically depressed variety and he found a certain solace in his darkened bedroom.

Faithfully, Dave made excuses for him, keeping the judge at bay and the Slaughter boys busy with lots-to-do, busy makework. Dave was comforted knowing it wouldn't occur to the Bubbas to ask if anything were amiss because, for them, it was another work day, another day at the office. He suspected judge Canfield knew what was going on, but he also suspected the judge knew better than to make demands or to interfere with Eden at this point.

Since Alna went back to check on her designer business, Dave was back with a vengeance. Each morning he walked what he called "the perimeter" and, weather permitting, stood watch outside for hours at a time.

He'd returned from his morning walk and watch and was busy in the kitchen noisily making coffee and toast. For him, breakfast was coffee, black and his toast, almost as black, with a dab of butter and strawberry jam. Dave had finished buttering his slice of toast when a bleary-eyed Eden, wakened by the activity, appeared in the bedroom door.

"Anything shaking out there?" he asked, nodding to the kitchen door.

"Not much," Dave said, "I been keeping my eye on the north east corner though. I thought it looked for a while like deer were bedding down there, but now it looks more like someone's been messing around. Found a candy bar wrapper out there today. Never heard of that kind of candy before. The wrapper is red and white and says 'Gaze…' on it. Some of it is torn off. Got any idea what kind of candy bar starts out 'Gaze?'"

"Probably some kid fooling around," offered Eden who ignored the question.

"Probably some kid playing with himself," Dave replied. "I'll check that area at a different time and see if I can catch a glimpse of whoever is eating Gaze… bars out there.

"You gonna' go to work today?"

"What time is it?"

"Some time after 10:00, I think."

Eden stretched, picked up a piece of uneaten toast, took a bite, spit it out into his hand and tossed it in the waste basket.

"You eatin' that shit? It's burnt," he complained.

"Thought you liked it that way. You gonna' go to work?"

"Maybe later this afternoon if I can find the energy."

"Here, drink some of this battery acid," Dave said handing him a mug of vile looking black coffee. "It'll get you right up and running—if you don't have a heart-attack first."

Eden took a tentative sip and smiled. "I like it strong, but this you could cut with a knife. Should wake the dead, maybe it'll get me started at least."

"What say we go in to the office? I need to get some paperwork done that I've been putting off for quite a while. You know, I knew I was never cut out to be the boss. Without someone on my ass, I just tend to drift along. I don't think I'm gonna' even try to get re-elected. I wouldn't even think about it if someone else would run and promise to hire me as their deputy. I've always been more of the deputy type. I just never wanted to run things."

"Well, you know better than to think I might do it. You're a swell fellow and all, but being sheriff—and most of all, being a deputy is a pure shit job," complained Dave.

"Hey, I could write a book so don't get me started. Let's get off our butts and get to the office before someone catches on to the fact we have easy jobs."

Chapter 29

At the same time Eden and Dave arrived at the office in Rainelle, Joey Dulaney pulled off the dirt road on the bluff behind Eden Whitloe's Random Creek home. He drove a short distance up an old logging road to a point where he could proceed no further.

Like some disco fog machine, his breath clouded the crisp, late winter air as he filched through the clutter of the back seat of the old Malibu. He finally found the rifle and what was left of a box of cartridges. Noticing his box of candy bars was half empty; he stuck a fresh goody in his jacket pocket, slammed the door and trudged toward a familiar spot. He didn't have the feeling of excitement he expected. So far, this was just another day, another walk in the park.

This would be an excellent stand for a deer drive, thought Joey as he surveyed the scene below. It wasn't exactly what one might call a sniper's nest, but it was good enough. There was a new fence post with a board nailed to it that would serve as an excellent rest for the rifle and the field of fire was completely clear, not so much as a weed to deflect a bullet.

No car in the drive, no activity around the house. However, this excellent, cold, clear day was not to be the day. He would have to return later that evening. The light might not be as good, but everything else would be superb. The wind would be non-existent and with no wind, the shot would be even easier. *Too easy, maybe I should come back when it would be more of a challenge.*

When Joey returned to the fence post position later that afternoon, the sun was a blurry burst behind a copse of maple trees that cast long shadows down across Random Creek hollow. About halfway between the crest of the bluff the sun had cut a dividing line in the hollow bathing one side of it in fiery late afternoon sunlight and the other with the beginnings of a cool evening dusk.

On the way home, Eden had dropped Dave off at his service station/shop in Brightbrook. He told Eden that he would take his delivery truck to work the following day and give the sheriff a much-appreciated evening to himself.

Eden drove up to his home alone while the lone gunman was scanning his front yard with a shiny new telescopic sight. He would have to act quickly to get a shot off while the sheriff was walking the few feet from his pickup to the front door.

Joey mused about leaving a card on his kill, a card that would be similar to the view through the scope, the symbol of the new Zodiac killer, something that would confound and confuse the cops, something to tell the world that an icy-nerved serial killer was lurking in the Pennsylvania woods. After today, he would be famous—a celebrity.

"… But I shot a man in Reno just to watch him die…"

A line from Johnny Cash's "Folsom Prison Blues" had recently become his own, personal earworm, squirming through his mind and clinging to his brain. This would be his first vengeance killing, his first male victim—cold shit.

Below, Eden was still inside the cab of the truck. Joey had no way of knowing Eden was going through the daily mail, looking for bills and—hopefully—checks. While he sorted through the mess, he listened as his favorite law-and-order talk show host on the truck's radio. The host explained how a bartender had escaped being robbed and claimed the fact that the bartender was armed with a .357 magnum had saved his bacon. Eden sat a moment longer picking up on the latest gory details.

Above, Joey fidgeted and waited for the sheriff to exit the truck cab. His view of the truck window blurred and refocused in the crosshairs of the scope as his finger nervously stroked the trigger guard. Should he dare touch the sliver of metal that would send hot gas down the barrel and propel the bullet on its way?

Suddenly, without warning, the sheriff opened the door and was standing beside the cab. He ducked down for a second to put something back in the truck, the quick motion causing Joey's heart to leap but once again Eden stood full erect, a target silhouetted against the bright background created by the afternoon sun.

"Well I know I had it coming, I know I can't be free…," moaned Johnny from somewhere inside Joey's head. Except for the twitter of a few birds, it was quiet, quiet until the crack of a rifle split the Pennsylvania woodland.

The shooter's scope revealed the target had dropped—almost in slow motion—unimpeded, like a stone in a pool as complete silence reigned. It also revealed an arterial stream that confirmed it was an unquestionable kill.

Chapter 30

Enrico Moratti and Jimmy Henderson had no idea of the effect they had on Andy Walbridge. The meeting was short, if not sweet and it left Andy with the definite feeling that if he didn't do exactly as he was instructed, he would join a growing list of former Rigdonite cultists. He knew full well that no one left the group willingly or alive.

Since Randy Winter was found shot to death in a motel room in upstate New York, Andy had been considering leaving everything and running. The only problem—where was he to run? They, whoever *they* might be, would track him down and... It was too horrible to contemplate so he tried not to think about it.

Rico began, "We are from up in New York. I think you know where, so I'm not going into a lot of detail. I know also that you know who sent us. Right?"

When there was no response from Andy, Rico shouted, "RIGHT?"

"Yeh, I think so," Andy responded hesitantly, "I suppose I do."

Jimmy let Rico do all the talking. He was there for atmosphere and presence and he was doing his part very, very well.

"The big guy from upstate's got a job for you. Nothing personal, you understand, business. Ain't nothing to think about, nothing you can say no to, so let's say it's a proposition you can't refuse. Oh I suppose you could refuse this job," he said with a smirk, "But then you'd have to take a ride back up with us—in the trunk. Know what I'm sayin'?"

Jimmy chuckled and smiled his intimidating smile. When he caught Andy glancing his way, he patted his side where it was obvious there was a gun under his jacket.

"Okay, okay, I've always done what I was told. You tell me what has to be accomplished and you can consider it done," Andy whined.

"You got a gun?" asked Rico.

"No."

"Bullshit. All you rednecks down here got guns. You start messing around with me and…"

"I don't have a gun, but I have a rifle," Andy responded quickly.

"Ah now mister wise-ass is splitting hairs with us, Jimmy. Look, if you want to mess with me, I'll let Jimmy there straighten you out and you ain't gonna' like it one bit."

"I have a deer rifle. I'm not very good with it, but I have one," Andy pleaded.

"Good boy, that's even better. Get a box or two of shells and practice up. You can shoot from a distance and that way you make a clean get away—if you are half-assed smart, that is."

"What is it you want me to do?"

"No, not what, who."

"Okay," Andy said hopelessly, "who is it you want me to do?"

"That's more like it. You guys down here have screwed the pooch. This is so messed up I don't know if it will ever get straightened away. It seems to our boss there is one person down here who might be able to blow the whistle on our whole organization. You got any idea who that might be?"

"The new sheriff, Eden Whitloe," Andy offered almost too quickly. "Shit, you want me to kill the sheriff, don't you?"

"Good boy," Rico said condescendingly. "He's a real smarty-pants, ain't he James?" He said as he reached over and patted Andy's cheek.

"Real smart," said Jimmy, speaking for the first time.

"Nothing to it," said Rico. "You go out to the sheriff's place and wait for him to show up. Blow his freakin' brains out, get in your car and drive home. Oh, you might want to set yourself up with an alibi first, there's sure to be someone that'll be askin' questions about it, a sheriff getting snuffed kinda' gets folk's attention, ya know. No reason they should suspect you, is there?"

"No. No reason at all."

"Good. You're a good boy." Rico patted his cheek once again. "You wouldn't like a trip to New York in our trunk anyway. Awful cramped back there—if you could feel anything."

"When?" asked Andy.

"Give us a few days to get clear, then you decide. If I don't read about a certain George County Sheriff being mysteriously shot by a sniper in the next few days, we'll be back to take you on that little ride I was telling you about."

"Is next week okay?"

"Sounds good. Good boy," Rico said patting his cheek in farewell. Holding up one finger he reminded Andy, "Practice, practice, practice."

In a few short minutes Andy had learned to hate Enrico Moratti more than anyone he ever knew. He didn't care all that much for Jimmy either.

* * * *

When Andy got to Dulaney's Hardware, he thought about buying a cheap brand of ammo for his rifle. After all, it was just for practice. Upon further consideration, he figured he should practice with the real stuff. Who knew, there could be a difference that might throw him off.

The Hardware owner, Carl Dulaney, hadn't waited on

customers since his son Joey had confessed to the murders of the Pretty Maidens so a young man who was a college student waited on Andy.

"I'd like a couple of boxes Remington .30-30 shells," he told the clerk.

"You want 150 grain or 170?"

"Huh?"

"150 or 170 grains? That's how much the bullet weighs. We got 'em in both."

This puzzled Andy, but he figured the bigger the better. It seemed reasonable to him a heavier bullet would have more killing power. Now he was glad he didn't opt for the off-brand. He remembered Remington often had Core-Lockt® in the description of their ammunition, so without a clue what Core-Lokt® meant, he asked the clerk for two, twenty round boxes of 170 grain Core-Lokt® shells.

By this time the kid behind the counter had Andy figured for a green horn, but had decided not to rub it in. The sale was made and Andy left the store with a brown paper bag and a wallet $40.83 lighter. As he strolled down Main Street, he pondered the high price of murder. *Never thought of it as being this expensive,* he thought as he headed out to the game lands to practice using the rifle.

* * * *

This is how it came to pass that Joey Dulaney and Andy Winter happened to be on the ridge above Eden Whitloe's Random Creek home on a cold afternoon. The planets must have been aligned because they not only happened to be near the same place at the same time, they were there for exactly the same purpose.

Joey was oblivious to Andy's presence. Pretending to be a hunter, Andy had walked from the other side of the ridge. When he came to the top of the ridge, he instantly recognized Joey who had placed his rifle on the board in front of him so that he could view the valley below.

Holy shit, thought Andy, he's lining up a shot to take out the sheriff. He suddenly realized his task was being done for him. Relief welled up. He could wait until Joey finished his handiwork, then take out the fugitive Joey with one shot and become the hero of George County in one fell swoop. He almost pissed himself in anticipation and joy. It was almost too good to be true.

He could see the newspapers now...

Chapter 31

A stiletto of light pierced a stone wall and found its way slowly across the bruised face of an unconscious Hope Heflin. She was convinced it was the light of near death experience she had heard so much about. Was she dead or near death? Was this the way it would be for eternity?

If this was *it* for her, it would be fine. There was calm and serenity, a sensation of floating above her body and all was moving toward a lighted passageway. In the background there was a trickling sound of water that grew and rushed and roared through her head. It became as loud as Niagara bringing a crescendo of pain as it faded to a trickle once again. Her head felt near to exploding.

As her head began to clear, she began to come to her senses and finally realized she was in the springhouse, the place Joey had told her about, the place she had gone for water. Fortunately, the spring, now frozen over, was no longer flowing into the stone tray—fortunately because Hope was lying face down in it and she had no idea how she got there.

Bit by bit her memory of last night began to return. She remembered feeling good and Joey screaming in what she believed at the time was ecstasy. Her hand touched her bruised lip as she recalled his hand over her mouth, then over her nose—she couldn't breathe or beg him to stop. She felt her throat. She couldn't remember the details, but at some point he had taken his hands from her nose and mouth and placed them around her neck. First an inky black, a sudden burst of white light, then—nothing until now.

Sitting there with both hands on her throat, she spoke a sudden realization to no one, "The bastard tried to kill me." *Who would have imagined it. The little creep actually tried to take me out.*

Hope was colder than she could ever remember. The springhouse protected her from the wind, but it was only a few degrees above freezing. She didn't know what hypothermia was, but her body did and she knew if she didn't get to somewhere where it was warm, Joey's mission would be accomplished.

She crawled through the slush and made her way to the shack, collapsing inside the door. Inside wasn't much warmer than the springhouse. With an effort she didn't know was in her, she found the cube heater and turned it full force on her hands and arms. After she warmed a little, using the quilts and blankets she fashioned a tent under the table and pulled the cube heater in with her. At that point consciousness slipped away once moreShe lost track of time, but awakened again, this time she felt much too warm. She found some scraps of unfinished meals she and Joey had eaten and now nourished, if not completely restored, she began to think of revenge.

A natural feeling of getting even gave way to an all-consuming need. As she saw it, she had no other reason for being. After a few hours of lying around, getting herself together, a plan began to take shape. Hope was fully aware that she was not thinking rationally, but she was also aware that this was quite normal for her. Where an average person might consider getting away and hiding out for a time, she could only think of the manner in which she would kill Joey Dulaney. After all, she reasoned, she was a natural born killer. It was her life's purpose, her reason for existence.

She recalled their plan for killing the deputy that had helped put Joey in jail. She obsessed about being a sniper.

Yes, a sniper in a Ghillie suit, crawling, invisible, unseen, camouflage-painted face, rifle wrapped with burlap, crawling toward an unsuspecting target to deliver one shot, a bullet that the bastard Joey would never hear. His head would snap forward and a piece of his skull would fly out just like in that grainy 8mm Zapruder film. It would serve two purposes, vengeance and celebrity. She would be famous like that Russian woman sniper in WWII she had seen on the History Channel. The woman on the History Channel had 309 kills to her credit including 36 enemy snipers. Now there was a woman with balls.

* * * *

Unfortunately Roscoe Poncett lived only a couple of miles from the hideout cabin Joey and Hope had been using. It was his misfortune to be the one person Hope Heflin would encounter on her search for a vehicle, money, sustenance and a rifle.

The morning was damp and cold with no hint of warmer weather. Hope had no idea what to expect when she approached the derelict camp trailer that was the home of Roscoe Poncett. If she could have seen herself, she might have given up on the notion of approaching anyone. Her face was dirty and bruised and under a filthy quilt she used as a shawl, she wore little more than her underwear. She did make sure she took her trusty knife with her, just in case she met up with Joey Dulaney on the road. She did know how to use a knife, she had practical experience.

Roscoe lived alone and apparently sustained himself on a Social Security check, road kill and whatever game or vegetation happed to be in season. He wasn't above stealing a chicken now and then or taking something from a local farmer's field. He grew some dope and sold what he didn't smoke to the local kids. The neighbors saw the septuagenarian as more of a nuisance than the eccentric he was. Even before the hippies moved into Brightbrook, Roscoe had dropped out and dropped into the western end of the county. If anyone asked him what he did for a living he told them he was a Druid priest. Very few asked and no one had ever tried to pursue the matter with him.

He had no way of knowing his luck was running thin when he answered a slap on his trailer door.

Chapter 32

"Watcha' want?" asked Roscoe.

Roscoe didn't normally open his door to find a bedraggled teen-age girl standing there, but normally, he didn't have visitors of any sort.

"I'm cold and hungry. Could you spare something to eat?"

Her words came out as if from a stranger's larynx. She sounded like Regan MacNeil's demon voice done by Mercedes McCambridge in the *Exorcist*. (Neither Hope or Roscoe had any idea who Mercedes McCambridge was.)

Hope was beginning to wish she had gone further down the road. The inside of the trailer was everything one might imagine and more. It smelled of burnt pork, cannabis and the faint odor of shit. However, she was in no position to be choosey.

"Sure," said Roscoe. "Come on in. You look like somthin' the dogs been fightin' over. Betcha' had a fight with your old man."

"You mean my daddy?"

"Naw, your husband, boyfriend—like that. Looks like you got in a fight and I figger he kicked your butt out the door. Is that about what happened?"

"You got it right away, that's exactly what happened. We were staying in an old shack down the road a-piece and—well, I guess we got on each other's nerves. Cabin fever, you might say.

"If I can stay here over night, he'll probably be over his snit by morning and everything'll be all right and I can go back. At least I hope that's what will happen. He's real mad right now though and I'm afraid to go back there tonight," Hope told him.

"I ain't fitted out much for company, 'specially where a lady is concerned. Dinner table lets down into a bed. I reckon you can sleep there if you want."

"Looks real nice to me. I think you're fitted out about right. Looks downright homey," Hope said, thinking, *what a shit hole.*

"Got some clothes that look like they'll fit you if you like. A neighbor gave me some work pants and a long-sleeve shirt for Christmas a couple of years back. Never out of the box. Got an old denim jacket you can have to. It ain't so nice, but it'll keep you warm."

"About that food—something smells real good."

You like possum? I got one in the pot back there cookin' in some kinda' greens I froze fer keepin' last summer, put some ramps in there too."

Hope wondered where he might have gotten a possum in mid winter, but decided it wouldn't be wise to even ask. Hungry as hell, cold and miserable and her finely tuned sensibilities not allowing her to refuse, she lied to Roscoe. "I'd love some—um possum."

"Really? You really like possum? I was just shittin' ya'. I got a chicken in that pot—makin' soup just as soon as I throw some noodles in with it."

Hope settled in behind the fold-down table while Roscoe ladled out soup for her.

"Soon as you get some of old Roscoe's soup in you, you'll warm right up and be right as rain.

"You not having any?" she asked.

"Not right now. You eat all you want. If there's not enough, I'll put some more water in and make more."

It may not have been the world's best, but Hope was in no position to judge. To her it was the best meal she ever had.

Roscoe busied himself making paths through the clutter and tidying up as best he could. He couldn't do much about the old-man aroma that consisted of fried pork, pot, snuff, urine and B.O., but as time passed, Hope didn't seem to notice it as much.

Out of nowhere, Hope found herself asking Roscoe if he was a dirty old man. He lifted one arm and took a whiff of well-ripened pit and said, "yep! About as dirty as they come I reckon."

"You know what I mean. You're making fun of me aren't you?"

"I suppose it's not that I wouldn't like to be—ah active. You see all that passed me by a few years ago. I can't afford no Viagra stuff, 'sides there's no one around to get it up for. So I just kind of ignore all that. You got nuthin' to fear from me. I'll not bother ya' none. I appreciate the company though."

"When I gotta' go, where do I go?"

"Oh." Roscoe said, not catching her meaning at first. "There's a bathroom right behind you. No running water. I keep a bucket in there in the winter. Go outside most of the time in the warm weather. You gotta' go, go in there. Just remember the old rule."

"Yeh," said Hope, "if it's brown flush it down. If it's yellow, let it mellow."

Roscoe laughed a geezer's laugh. "You're something else. That boyfriend'll be right after you come morning.

"Tell you what, if you want a bath, I'll heat up a bucket of water and you can take one in the tub. You might want to scrub it out a little first though."

* * * *

After she emerged from the bathroom, Hope found Roscoe making a bed out of the dining table. The covers were no better than the ones at the shack, but they weren't much worse either.

She made an attempt to wash her underwear while taking a bath and hung her things on the back of the bench near the stove.

Without much ado, she crawled into the bed and pulled a quilt under her chin. Roscoe sat there on the edge of the bed for a moment. *Oh yuck, what do I do if he tries to kiss me goodnight.* She squeezed her eyes shut as he reached out and gently pulled the quilt up around her.

"It's going to be all right little gal. Don't worry about a thing. Old Roscoe will be in the next room. You need anything at all, you just give a holler. And don't worry about your feller either. If he shows up I'll handle it. I got a way of dealin' with fightin' folks.

As Roscoe turned out the light and headed for his bedroom, Hope asked. "Roscoe? You still there."

"Ain't goin' nowhere."

"Roscoe, do you have a gun?"

"All rednecks in these parts got guns. Now good night, we can talk in the morning."

Chapter 33

Hope found that sleep was slow in coming. She lay awake for what seemed to be hours, her mind filled with plans for vengeance. She would have to wait to see what sort of firearm Roscoe might produce. If it was a pistol, that would take a different plan of attack than if it were a rifle or shotgun. She was placing her bets on a shotgun, but decided to put off plans for Mr. Dulaney until morning.

The matter of planning what to do with Mr. Roscoe was a problem she would mull over tonight. She found a place within herself that hated the thought of killing him, but any plan to leave him alive just wouldn't come. She sincerely appreciated his help and willingness to let her share his food and stay with him—could it be that she was developing a fondness for the rancid old shit?

These sorts of thoughts had to be banished from her mind. They were ill suited for a real natural born killer. Mickey and Mallory Knox would have never allowed sentiment to enter their thoughts—to warm their ultimate coolness—to take away their edge. It was something she would have to work on through the night, she thought to herself as she drifted off imagining Roscoe in the role of an evil stepfather. This wasn't such a far reach for Hope.

* * * *

Sometime around 9:30 she awoke to the sizzle and smell of

frying bacon.

"Thought you was going to sleep all day," said Roscoe in the way of a morning greeting.

"Gotta take a leak," Hope announced as she threw back her quilt and headed for the rear of the trailer. While Roscoe was occupied and she was near his bedroom door she ventured a peek inside.

Holy shit! She exclaimed to herself. Inside the bedroom was a workshop—not an ordinary workshop, but a gunsmith's workbench. Stacked around it were piles of firearms of every sort. There were revolvers, automatic pistols, rifles of various kinds and shotguns. A Weatherby Vanguard Sporter SS .30-06 equipped with a Unertl sniper scope was mounted on the bench.

Hope jumped as she heard Roscoe behind her. "You ought not be messin' where you ain't invited. You can get yourself in a whole lot of trouble that-a-way, you know," he said when he saw she was aware of his presence.

Hope didn't quite know what to say. "Oh, I was looking for a... uh... towel," she blurted in a feeble attempt to cover her embarrassment at being caught in the act of snooping.

Dropping the redneck, good-old-boy tone, he began speaking in relatively perfect English. "I work as a subcontractor fixing weapons for some people—people I don't even know. I do know, however, if they knew you were snooping, you might not make it through the day.

Resuming his redneck coot persona Roscoe said, "I shure hope I ain't gonna' haveta' tell anybody you wuz here. That you wuz snoopin' around."

Suddenly the warmth Hope had been feeling for the old man cooled—replaced by ice water. Maybe this is what it truly meant to be cool.

"Now I fixed you a breakfast, so you sit down and eat, then gather up what I gave you and get your punk ass on down the road," Roscoe said harshly.

As she ate, she planned what to do from this point on. Roscoe had cleared her thoughts and her new, cool mind worked overtime. Now her thoughts were centered on what to do to rid herself of him. If they found the old coot with a bullet in his body, there would be hell to pay. There would be a murder investigation and things could get hairy. An arranged suicide wasn't any good either. It would raise red flags, especially when they found him dead among all of those weapons. Her weapon of choice was her knife. She was experienced with it and knew what it could do. Better yet, she knew what she was capable of with it in her hands.

Hope finished her breakfast and went to the opposite side of the table, behind Roscoe, where she moved a pan around on the small stove. Roscoe caught a glimpse of Hope and her knife in the reflection of a cabinet door and instinctively knew what she was up to. He pulled his collar down with both hands and said, "go ahead. I know what you're up to. I'm ready to go. I thank you in advance."

She was in mid knife-stroke and her cool, calculating self was frozen in mid air, shattered by Roscoe's invitation. Too late though, too late to stop now. Roscoe sat as if he wasn't even aware of the slit that ran through his unkempt beard from one of his ears to the other.

Like the others Hope had slaughtered, there was lots of blood, but she had grown used to it. She was cool. Maybe that's what folks meant when they said a person was cold blooded.

She quickly looked around for a backpack, a suitcase or anything she could carry some stuff in. She found a gunnysack and rigged it with ropes to use as shoulder straps.

That day she carried whatever she could and stashed it under the shack she and Joey had occupied. The first item of choice was the Weatherby rifle and four boxes of .30-06 shells.

By the time she had made a couple of trips to the trailer, shadows were lengthening and cold air was settling in. If there was a fire now, it would light the night sky and attract too much attention. She could wait until the following day— Roscoe wouldn't be going anywhere.

* * * *

Hope didn't know much about bottled gas except for the fact that she had been warned about its dangers, over and over. She knew that Roscoe's trailer was heated with propane and his cook stove used it as well. There were small cylinders of the stuff stored inside the place and a larger storage cylinder was hooked onto the front of the trailer.

She checked the bedroom/workshop and as she suspected there were several containers of gunpowder stored there. All she could think of was BOOM as she set to work gathering combustible material and stuffing it under the trailer. When she had enough piled up, she went to the kitchen and turned on all the burners on the stove to high. Patting Roscoe's body, she said, "have a high old time. Hope I don't see much of you around anymore."

Trailer fires are notorious killers and except for the secondary explosions, this one would be like all the rest. Nothing to examine but what was left of the bones of an old man and a few bits of metal frame that survived the heat. With hardly any luck at all, there wouldn't be much to investigate. Just another careless derelict caught in a fire of his own making.

A match, and a brief flutter of the flame as it struggled to ignite some newspaper, then some cardboard and next some plastic. Soon there was a respectable fire under the trailer and Hope was off and running back to her cabin in the woods where she waited for the explosion that was sure to come.

Just when it seemed as if the trailer and its contents would never explode, there was a tremendous ball of flame that shot skyward and a few milliseconds later a thunderous explosion Hope could have never imagined. Next there were some smaller booms, then smaller explosions and finally a series of pops that must have been individual rounds of ammunition going off. It was nearly half an hour when the George County Volunteer Fire Department arrived to survey the scene. What they found was believed to be the bones of the trailer dweller and a few bits of metal frame that survived the heat.

* * * *

Later, that evening Hope Heflin took the .30-06 rifle from its hiding place and examined it carefully. She jacked open the bolt and learned about its interior workings. She closed the bolt, slamming it shut with the heel of her hand as she had seen others do and holding it into position against her cheek, pulled the trigger. Next she took one of the bullets from a box of shells and inserted it into the firing chamber. She raised the rifle once again and this time peeked through the telescopic sight. It was aimed at the side of the shack. She didn't want to miss and wanted to know exactly where the bullet would hit. She was determined to become the equal of any sniper in learning the weapon. She might not be aware of the niceties of windage and elevation and the subtleties of ballistics, but she would only need one well-placed shot.

Chapter 34

Dave and Eden had just gotten settled in at the office and were going through stacks of paper, mostly garbage that had accumulated in their in-baskets. A warm spell had graced the county and outside, it was invitingly sunny. The men wished to be anywhere but behind their desks.

Somewhere in the background a phone was ringing with its incessant boop, boop, boop. Eden tried to get phones that had good old-fashioned ringers, but the only ones available had electronic boopers.

"I hate those soulless phone ringers almost as much as I hate mall music," mumbled Eden as Dave took the call.

"We might as well have stayed home, seems like everything happens out on the western end these days," Dave offered.

"Why? What's up?"

"Had a trailer fire out near the West Virginia state line last night. A fatality and they want us to take a look."

"Horizontal or vertical?"

"What?"

"Which state line? The one on the southern edge or the one that runs north?"

"Oh. Close to both, I reckon. Somewhere near Quiet Dell."

"I'll check with the VFD boys and get a fix on it. You want to tag along for company, you're welcome," offered Eden.

The first part of the trip was a familiar one, but as they

headed toward the middle of nowhere, the sheriff consulted a county map, somewhat annoyed that they were having to go on a goose chase out to the end of the earth to look over some ashes left by some careless trailer dweller.

"What'd they say his name was?" asked Eden.

"Uh," Dave looked at his clipboard. "Roscoe—uh, Roscoe Poncett. Unusual name for this area, don't you think?"

"Guess so. Doesn't sound familiar to me. I know most of the folks out this way but don't know any Poncetts. Probably some old hermit goofball smoking in bed. I don't know why anyone does that shit, you'd think people would learn."

"Yeah, this is a pain in the ass, but it's a great day to get out of the office don't you think?"

"You got that right. I get squirrely when it's nice out and I get stuck in there."

After getting lost twice and consulting the map a few times they finally pulled onto a gravel road leading to the remains of the trailer—or rather—where the trailer had been. There was a VFD pickup standing by in case of a flare-up and the Medical Examiner's van was parked nearby. The Medical Examiner and Coroner were the same person—Dr. Vinnie. A geeky looking college intern accompanied the good doctor.

"Hey Doc," said Eden.

"Hey Eden. Hi Dave," replied the M.E.

"You getting' ready to bag him up?"

"Yeh, you want a look-see before we move what's left? Ain't much to see. Even some of the bones are burned up and some must have blown away in the explosion. Make that explosions."

"Propane?"

"That's my guess, but he must have been a re-loader. Lots of powder and casings around—and a whole bunch of guns. Must have been a collector or tinkerer."

Eden and Dave moved to where they had a better view of the remains so they could make a show of examining the scene.

"Seen enough?" Eden whispered to Dave who was taking notes so it would look like he was doing something.

"Saw more than enough before I got here."

The Sheriff caught Dr. Vinnie's attention, "not much we can do here. We'll go back and file a report. You want to see it?"

"I don't think so. If something comes up later, you can send me a copy. Looks like Andy's bought hisself another cremation. No sense putting this one in a nice oak casket," the M.E. said absently, in his usual insensitive manner.

The trip back passed through Brightbrook, so they stopped at Dave's place for a donut and a Coke.

"Sure hope no one catches us eating donuts on duty," said Dave.

"Why? What?"

"It's a cop thing, you wouldn't understand."

"Very funny. You know, sometimes you really crack me up… not."

"You make a connection between Roscoe's bones out there and the pretty maiden's?"

"You're really workin' overtime to piss me off, aren't you?"

"No, I just wondered—you know, you're the one making connections. I just wondered."

"No connection. Not even remote, just a careless old coot that cooked himself. I don't think he had any family, but maybe someone will claim him. I can't see any links between this and any of that other stuff—unless…"

"Unless what?"

"Unless he was a Rigdonite."

Chapter 35

Although Delwyn Brody never liked his name, his Second Wife always assured him it sounded distinguished. His other wives never mentioned it. He never liked the title Illustrious Leader either but his Third Wife thought it was "dreamy." It was too 19th Century, too—well, it sounded, dumb, like something from a kid's comic book. He was stuck with it though. It was part of the history, tradition that was set in stone by Dr. Rigdon. Changing it would be heresy of the first order.

Brody—he preferred using his last name—did enjoy the authority of the office though. He liked issuing orders particularly when he was directing the demise of one of the members. It filled him with a satisfying sense of power. Power was a preciously limited commodity where he worked. He was usually on the other end of a boss's power trip so it was especially sweet when he used it.

Inquisitor—it was another one of those archaic words, a position dreamed up by Dr. Rigdon. Brody found it in his Rolodex. There was no name for the office holder. That was unknown even to him. The purpose of the office was to keep everyone in the sect in line. The office was filled every four years by the drawing of lots. It was a position no one could refuse and one in which everyone, male and female had to serve. The duties of the office, duties that might have made Tomás de Torquemada wince, were contained in the final chapter of *The Book*.

From the area code and the first three digits of the phone number, Brody could guess the location. It was Rainelle, Pennsylvania.

"Hello."

"This is Mr. Brody."

"Sorry, you have a wrong number," the person hung up.

Brody pushed redial.

"I told you before, you have a wrong number."

"Do you know a number I could call?"

"Look in the back of *The Book*," the exasperated voice said and then the person hung up once again.

Brody opened a book lying on his desk and turned to the final chapter. Surely enough he found a phone number scrawled in the margin of the very last page. He figured it was a secure line and the person he had been talking with was extremely concerned about being exposed. He dialed the number.

"Hello."

"This is Mr. Brody, again."

"I hope this is important. I'm up to my ass in deep shit right now. I guess I don't have to tell you how badly all of this has been handled and I assume that's why you called. Look, I'm in no position to..."

By this time Brody' anger was aroused. Who was this upstart questioning his authority—his power. "I know you have a degree of anonymity that is there to protect you, however, you are a member and I can find out..."

"Are you threatening me?"

Brody could see the conversation was degenerating into a Bevis and Butthead routine that was going nowhere, so he backed off.

"Look, let's not go there. Believe me I understand your concerns," Brody said in a more conciliatory tone. "I just want you to look into a few things for me and report back. You won't open yourself to exposure, all you have to do is observe and report."

"As long as we understand each other. Tell me what you need."

"First the easy part. I have two gentlemen working in George County. Do you have a pen and paper?"

"Yes, go ahead."

"They are James Henderson and Enrico Moratti and they were selected by the council to do some clean-up work down there. You are probably familiar with their work by now."

"I know their work. They seem very efficient."

"Well, keep an eye on them and make sure I hear about any problems or slip ups."

"What else?"

"Mr. Henderson and Mr. Moratti were to contact a member and to give him an assignment. Do you know about this matter?"

"Yeh, they got hold of Andy Winter and told them he's to take out the sheriff down here. That's some risky shit, and I'm steering clear of that one."

Brody puffed himself up and barely in control of his anger, he laid it out for the Inquisitor. "Look, I don't know who you are—now. But believe me, I can find out. I need your cooperation."

"I…"

"Don't interrupt. I need your cooperation. I need progress reports on Mr. Winter's efforts and if something doesn't happen soon, I will expect you to assume his responsibilities."

The line was quiet.

"You still there?" asked Brody

"Yeh,"

"You know what will happen if you can't perform the duties of your office, so I'm not even going to get into it. Understand?"

"Fully. How often do you want reports?"

"I would appreciate it if you would send something today.

Use my email address, it's in your copy of The Book. Be sure to encrypt the message. Get back to me every couple of days as things progress."

"Anything else?"

"I hear there was a trailer fire out on the west end. Anything that should concern me."

"I don't think so. It was some old guy who was doing some gun repairs for me. Seems he got careless, smoking in bed or something. You can expect that sort of thing."

"If you think you can bring all of this to closure it will be much appreciated. If you have to get involved where the sheriff is concerned, please know your salary will be tripled."

"Good to know. Are we done?"

"I think so. Stay safe. Goodbye."

The line on the other end went silent.

* * * *

Reports

Shotgun reports can be adequately described as a boom. The firing of a rifle almost defies description. Some might call it a crack, others my say it's a bang. Only those who have fired one know the true sound of a high-powered rifle.

The reports echoed through the Pennsylvania woodlands as Hope Heflin fired round after round into a distant target. She was determined to become as proficient with the rifle as she could. Before her second box of shells, she was putting a round in a head-size target with regularity. With the second box, she increased the distance to 150 yards and was soon hitting the target every time. Through trial and error she learned how to adjust the scope for distance and wind.

She was ready, now to find Mr. Dulaney. It was reasonable to assume he would be going after Eden Whitloe, he surely seemed obsessive about exacting vengeance on the lawman so Hope decided to stake out his Random Creek home. She figured if she had the opportunity, she would take out the deputy as well as Joey. Two for the price of one, should cause a real shit storm in the county. The outlaw and the lawman taken out by an unknown assailant—perfect.

* * * *

In the military any coincidental events that occur at least three times are considered suspicious. The fact that three people were on the bluff above Eden's house was not a random occurrence. There was nothing random about the fact they were there to kill someone. Each had their own motivation and each had their target. If the circumstances were known, no one would have believed this was some freaky alignment of the stars—it was practically pre-destined. The outcome of the convergence, however was anything but predictable and strangely enough, the only person that could have been surprised, wouldn't be.

* * * *

It came to pass that Joey Dulaney and Andy Winter happened to be on the ridge above Eden Whitloe's Random Creek home on a cold afternoon. The planets must have been aligned because they not only happened to be near the same place at the same time, they were there for exactly the same purpose and, Hope Hathaway would be along shortly.

Joey was oblivious to Andy's presence. Pretending to be a hunter, Andy had walked from the other side of the ridge. When he came to the top of the ridge, he instantly recognized Joey who had placed his rifle on the board in front of him so that he could view the valley below.

Holy shit, thought Andy, he's lining up a shot to take out the sheriff. He suddenly realized his task was being done for him. Relief welled up. He could wait until Joey finished his handiwork, then take out the fugitive Joey with one shot and become the hero of George County in one fell swoop. He almost pissed himself in anticipation and joy. It was almost too good to be true.

He could see the newspapers now…

* * * *

Hope arrived a few minutes after Andy to see Joey lining his sights up on a target below them. The distance was about 150 yards, he was resting the rifle on a board nailed to a fence post. There was absolutely no wind and there were no small trees or weeds that might deflect the bullet. It was almost too easy and Joey never felt more relaxed as they all saw Eden's pickup turn in the drive.

Hope had positioned herself above and to the left of Joey. She didn't see Andy and Andy was oblivious to everything except the sniper in front of him. He sat with his rifle between his knees, the sling braced around his arms. At not much more than 100 feet, the crosshairs on his scope were hardly needed, but they were placed exactly on the back of Joey Dulaney's head.

Off to the left, her view of Andy blocked by a stand of large oak trees, she was leaning against a tree, bracing her rifle and taking aim at nearly the same spot as Andy.

Hope was the only one expecting the gun to fire. Even she didn't know the exact moment, because she had trained herself to squeeze the trigger and get off a round before she could flinch.

If he had a millisecond, he might have registered surprise but all he had was eternity. As it was Hope's scope revealed the target had dropped—almost in slow motion—unimpeded, like a stone in a pool as complete silence reigned. It also revealed an arterial stream that confirmed it was an unquestionable kill. Joey Dulaney would never kill again.

Below, Eden instinctively ducked and dashed to the cover of the house. *Damn,* he thought, more hunters or target practice. If this shit keeps up, I'm moving to town.

At first Andy wondered if his gun had fired prematurely, but it had not. He finally glanced over to where he suspected the shot originated and caught a glimpse of Hope, her rifle was held down at her side as she leaned against a tree. He instantly recognized that she was, in fact, the shooter and re-positioned himself until the cross hairs of his scope were filled with Hope's temple.

His target dropped—almost in slow motion. The scope revealed a scene of carnage that reminded him of the Zapruder film and for him, that confirmed it was an unquestionable kill.

He didn't get up for quite a while as he tried to wrap his head around what had happened. The ridge top had turned into a killing field. Two young people lay dead, like some kind of hunter's game. Undoubtedly both were killers, but how was the girl involved and why did she want to kill Joey?

When he finally arose, Andy clicked the safety off of his weapon and pointed it at point blank range at Joey's head wound and fired off a single round.

As the impact of the afternoon settled in, Andy realized he still had unfinished business with Eden Whitloe. But the sheriff was now inside his house and that business would have to wait for another day. And Andy realized there wouldn't be many more days.

Chapter 36

It must have been nearly midnight when Eden heard a rap on his door. In the distance he could hear sirens and the whup, whup, whup of a helicopter hovering somewhere overhead. Through his bedroom window he could see lights sweeping the hollow.

He got out of bed, slipped on a pair of jeans and open deck shoes and headed to the living room where he opened the front door.

"Hi sleepyhead, you county boys are used to nine-to-five hours aren't you?" It was the Chief of State Police for George County Dan Brackenridge.

Shielding his eyes from the bright helicopter's spot that was coming through the door, Eden asked, "What the hell is going on?"

"Someone called in a report about a young couple being killed out this way—oh, about a half-hour ago."

"I see the chopper is flying up over the ridge over there, you think that's where they are?"

"That's what the guy on the telephone said. The call was placed out at the truck stop on the Interstate, so you know how reliable that can be. They got a couple of outside pay phones and you can use one of them without leaving your car. We have no clue who might have that placed the call."

"Hold on for a second while I get my shit together and I'll go up there with you. No point in walking up, there's a road to an old gas well up about three-quarters of the way. My pickup's a four-wheel-drive, so we can take it. Save a lot of hiking."

After a ride up the road and a short walk, the pair arrived at where Joey Dulaney had been shot. A short distance away laid Hope Heflin.

"What a freakin' mess," exclaimed Eden. "We are getting to be the murder capital, now aren't we?"

"I hear Fox News is coming down to get in on this one. Should be quite a circus," said Dan.

"Guess I can give up on any election bid right now. Damn!"

"You can look around if you like and I'll take the truck down and pick up some of the Crime Scene Investigators. Looks like it might be murder-suicide to me though. Maybe we can sell it that way. You know, case closed."

"Not with my luck," exclaimed Eden. "You gotta' know you're working with one of the most jinxed guys around. I got a strong feeling on this. I think it's connected."

"Now Eden, there you go again. Everything's connected to your big murder case. You just can leave it alone can you?"

Eden didn't answer. "You take the truck and go pick up the CSI boys and I'll look around. I'll string some crime scene tape in case anyone stumbles along and I'll try not to screw anything up for them."

In a short while the Chief was back and tagging along were two investigators and their gear.

"You call in Dr. Vinnie already?" Eden asked.

"Yep. Should be here pretty soon."

"The male is Joey Dulaney, can't tell so much looking at what's left of his face, but I'm pretty sure that's him," said Dan.

"It's him alright, no doubt. You think the girl might be the one from Cameron that did those home invasions?"

"Can't tell much from what I can see, but I'd bet that's her. I've only seen pictures on her that came in electronically. You know what those things look like. I'll bet the two of them were hanging together. He might have even helped her out with the home invasions."

"Yeh, regular Mickey and Mallory," mumbled Eden.

"Who?"

"Nothing, just a couple I saw in a movie."

"I got if figured they hooked up in Cameron, stole her parent's car, committed a couple of robbery-murders for cash and were hiding out in the woods somewhere close by. What ya' think?"

"Sounds all neat and tidy to me. Think they got in an argument that went downhill?"

"If the CSI guys can support it, that's how I'm gonna' report it. Looks like one killed the other, then maybe in a fit of remorse, shot themselves."

Eden walked to the crest of the ridge and looked down. "Coulda' sworn I heard three shots, maybe one of them missed? One thing makes no sense at all."

"Yeh, what's that."

"Why here? What the hell were they doing up here?"

"I'm sure you have a theory, one of your connections."

"Dave and I believe someone has been coming up here, watching me and looking for an opportunity to take me out."

"Now Eden..."

"Don't now Eden me." 'Eden said angrily, "Dave was up here, found grass trampled down and he found a candy bar wrapper. Someone was up here and it makes a whole lot of sense that someone was Joey Dulaney."

Chapter 37

That evening Eden got a phone call from Andy Winter. He said he had some new information on the killings out at Eden's place.

"I was there, Eden."

"What?" Eden fairly shouted into the phone. "You were where?"

Andy told him that he was on the scene when the murders occurred. He told him that he found Joey taking aim at Eden at the bottom of the hill and as a sort of automatic reaction, shot him to prevent him from shooting the sheriff.

"I don't think I meant to shoot him, but he was all lined up ready to pull that trigger. I saw him move his finger from the trigger guard to the trigger. That's when my gun went off. I didn't realize I had squeezed down that hard. I didn't see the girl at first. She took a shot at me and didn't have time to think. I turned and shot her in self-defense. It was reflexes, Eden, I didn't want to die," he exclaimed.

"Okay, Okay, take it easy," Eden said reassuringly. "I believe you and I'm sure Dan Brackenridge will believe you. There's only one thing—"

"What's that Eden? I told you everything."

"Think about this carefully. Tell me like you might tell a jury."

"Oh shit Eden, I think I need a lawyer."

"Not yet, Andy. You aren't charged with anything, there's no reason to worry if you are telling me the truth. You are telling me the truth, aren't you Andy?"

"Yes, I am."

"Tell me one thing then. What the hell were you doing out there?" Eden challenged him.

Andy hesitated long enough to arouse Eden's suspicions further. "I was checking the area out for hunting."

"Deer season's over Andy."

"I, I know. I was just checking it for next year and for other game. Mostly I was taking a hike, just to get away from things. You know business hasn't been all that good...

"Andy, why did you have a high powered rifle with you. Most people might take a pistol or a .22, but a deer gun? Come on."

Eden could sense that Andy was rattled. He explained that he took the rifle because it had a telescopic sight and he wanted to get a view through it to see what the field would look like. This wasn't unheard of and it lent a degree of credibility to his story.

"Andy, it's late and maybe you want some time to think things over. You sleep on it and come in first thing in the morning and I'll take your statement. I'll talk things over with the State Police and Judge Canfield and we'll see what they want to do. I think that when a death's involved, there has to be some sort of hearing or inquest, something like that, but if what you're telling me is the truth, it shouldn't amount to much."

Eden wasn't sure what to believe at this point. He figured that if Andy were given enough time and enough rope— He knew that Andy was a full fledged member of the Fundamentalist Rigdonites, but he didn't know how he might have been involved in the cover-up of the death of Myra Kinchloe. He was certain he couldn't be trusted and suspected Mr. Winter wasn't telling the whole truth.

Chapter 38

"Good morning Mr. Sleepyhead, you country boys are used to nine-to-five hours aren't you? And, I guess you can really sleep in when you're the boss."

Eden wasn't sure if it was a flashback, or exactly what was going on. He thought he heard the phone ring and he was pretty sure he had picked it up and said, "hello." Aside from that, he wasn't sure what time it was, or even what day it was for that matter. He glanced at the clock and found it was almost 11:30 a.m..

"Who is this?" Eden asked.

"It's Dave, Dave Quinn, you remember, Deputy Quinn. You drinkin' last night, Eden?"

"No, but I didn't get much sleep. You just woke me up and I'm kinda' groggy. What time is it?"

Dave decided it was better not to tell him to buy a watch and simply gave him the time.

"Ah, shit. I was supposed to be in there at nine. Has Andy Winter been in yet?

"Nope? You expectin' him?"

Eden told him to wait until he got to the office and they would talk about it. He would need the time of the drive to Rainelle to become fully awake.

An early-morning sun had ripped the frost loose from its grip on the valley as Eden slipped on his reflector shades to protect him from the now-overhead rays that were now doing damage to his headache.

It was past noon when Eden finally arrived at the
Sheriff's office in Rainelle. He promptly went to his desk and
summoned Dave on the intercom.

"Still no sign of Andy?" Eden inquired.

"Nope. What's up with Andy anyway?

Eden explained that Andy had called him last night with
his story about what had happened on the ridge above his
home. He filled Dave in on what he knew so far and that
he was expecting Andy to help him file a formal report this
morning.

"I wanted to get it all down and get Dan Brackenridge and
Judge Canfield in on it before we go any further down that
road."

"Good idea," said Dave. "You never know where Andy's
concerned. He's a real flake and might change his mind over
night. If you remember, he's one of those Rigdonites—at least
he was one."

"I'm not forgetting anyone who was involved in that mess.
As far as I'm concerned, they are still all Rigdonites, at least
the ones that are still alive. I'm getting worried that he might
have flown the coop though. His story sounded shaky to begin
with, now I'm thinking he was buying time."

"Are you thinking what I'm thinking?"

"Yeh, let's go over to the Walbridge Funeral home and see
if he's there. He should be back from lunch by now so we can
grab his ass—if he's still there."

* * * *

It was no wonder Andy's business was slow. The place
had all of the appeal of—well—a funeral parlor. The place
of business hadn't been refurbished in decades and Andy
relied on old family ties to keep things going. However, more
recently old families weren't cooperating.

The front door was locked and no amount of knocking
or calling could bring anyone to open it. "What now?" Dave

asked turning to Eden.

"Now I want you to come back at around 4:30 and check again. Same tomorrow. Check about every two or three hours. Maybe he'll turn up. I'm going to run over to his house, but he hasn't been returning calls, so I don't expect him to be at home. His family doesn't seem to know where he is, or they are dragging their feet protecting him."

"And if he doesn't show up..."

"Tomorrow afternoon, I'll put out an All Points on him and see if we can get him picked up. In the meantime, I'll see if I can get a search warrant so we can go into the funeral home and poke around. We'll have to dream up some things we are looking for though."

In the meanwhile Eden called the State Police to see if they had any information on Andy's whereabouts.

Dan Brackenridge had a strange question for him. "Eden did you or one of your guys pick up that Hope Heflin's rifle?"

"No, I assumed that you guys were in charge and left everything as it was. I know it was there when I rigged the tape. Weatherby, wasn't it?"

"Yeh, right, Weatherby Sporter SS. I remember seeing it—valuable gun—let's hope it's not stolen but we can't seem to find it anywhere. I know someone here must have picked it up. It's on the inventory, but I can't find it. I'll ask around tomorrow. It'll probably show up. I'll get an All Points Bulletin out and see if we can pick up Mr. Walbridge. Anything else?"

"Not that I can think of right now. Thanks."

Eden went to the courthouse and filled out the necessary paperwork for a search warrant. The main item on his list was a Weatherby Vanguard Sporter SS .30-06 rifle. Judge Canfield was out of town and since it didn't seem to be a life or death matter, Eden said he could pick the warrant up sometime tomorrow.

Chapter 39

"Hello."

"Are you free to talk?"

"Yes, go ahead."

"As you know, I normally avoid talking business on the phone. However, just when you think business down here is getting back to normal, things get worse."

"Go ahead, tell me about it."

"The guy you had on assignment gave it his best shot, if you get my meaning?"

"Yes."

"Well, it wasn't good enough. Blew it completely, now something else must be done. A new person and a new approach."

"What do you suggest?"

"Since my ass is way over the edge on this one, I'm going to take over from here. I'm the only one I trust...

"What about the two emissaries I sent down? Can't they handle things?

"Maybe they can, maybe they can't. I want you to call them off. See if they can find their way back up there, do anything to get them out of the county. And, get this straight, this isn't a proposal, or an offer, it's a demand. I'm taking over until this business is over and done with. I'm not taking any chance of having it mucked up any further."

"Do what you think is best. I'm sure you can handle it."

* * * *

Eden and Dave, armed with their search warrant and some burglary tools pulled into the Walbridge Funeral Home parking lot. The sky was overcast and even though it was late afternoon, it seemed like late evening. Perfect. Gloomy weather for breaking into the place. Eden didn't particularly like this part of sheriffing, and he disliked this particular assignment even more.

Dave went around the building, knocking at every door and shouting, "Sheriff's Department, open up."

As expected, there was no response from inside. As a last resort, the Sheriff slammed the door as hard as he could. With no response again, he chose a pry bar from his selection of tools and slipped it between the double doors. With very little effort, he popped both doors. *Nothing in there anybody would want anyway,* he thought as he entered and shouted out their presence.

They probed and poked for a couple of hours at which point Eden called for the Slaughter brothers to search the suspended ceilings in the individual parlor rooms. Searching for a rifle should be easier than trying to locate a handgun, but nearly all of the typical hiding places were empty.

Dave and Eden spent the rest of the afternoon and evening going through Andy's office and desk.

"I was hoping it wouldn't come to this, but I'm afraid we're going to have to get a search warrant for his house," said Eden. "I hate this shit. I really hate it. I figured he'd keep anything nefarious away from his home."

"Nefarious? Eden, you've been reading up on your thesaurus, getting ready for the election campaign?"

Since the shootings on the ridge over Random Creek, Dave insisted on staying with Eden for a few nights. Eden knew Dave was a person who wouldn't accept no for an answer and he invited him along on a trip to the supermarket.

When they arrived at Random Creek Dave suggested that he would walk the perimeter while Eden unloaded the groceries.

"Okay, there isn't that much stuff and I know where everything is supposed to go. Normally, I wouldn't let you off this easy, but I don't want you messing up my storage system."

Dave typically began at the corner of the fence line and walked to the top of the hill along the inside of the wire. He did it as much for the exercise as his real interest in checking things out but this time he was interested in seeing the ridge top where the killings had taken place one more time.

Don't suppose one of those numb-nuts state cops left the rifle up there? No, even they couldn't be that incompetent.

By the time he was halfway up the hill, he was out of breath and puffing, so he sat down for a rest. Viewing the house below, he once again imagined the sniper's nest on the ridge. It was a perfect location and he always thought that something should have been done to protect the driveway and entry to the house. *Maybe some trees and bushes.*

The evening shadows were lengthening and Dave knew there was only about an hour of daylight left, so he got up and pushed on to the top. In the dimming light, the place was spooky to begin with, but the knowledge that two people had recently been killed here, it was all the more creepy.

Dave looked around trying to imagine where they might have left the girl's rifle. It wasn't until he noticed some movement beyond the killing ground that his attention was drawn to it.

Now he was speaking aloud to himself, "What the... what the hell?" As he approached the moving form, it took shape. It was a human form that seemed to be hanging from a low tree branch.

"Holy shit!" he exclaimed aloud.

As he got closer, he recognized the person who was swaying gently in the evening breeze, a knot cutting into the neck, the face blue, eyes bulging and the tongue protruding slightly. The rope slowly twisted as the body revolved, then untwisted, causing the light behind to come and go.

In the corner of his eye he caught the glint of a metallic object, which on closer inspection looked to be a badge or insignia of some sort. He couldn't make it out in the failing light and without his reading glasses, so he thoughtlessly stuck it in a pocket.

Probably dropped by one of the dip shit investigators.

Chapter 40

"Hello."

"Are Henderson and Moratti back in New York by now?"

"How kind of you to inquire. Yes they are back and seem pleased that you have elected to take over their responsibilities. They know full well what will happen if our efforts down there are botched again."

"With the kind of people you've chosen be involved in this business, it's no wonder it's been screwed up from the beginning."

"Ah…"

"Before you start to protest, your boy, Andy Walbridge is now on the list. First he messed up his assignment and now he's missing. Don't you dare interfere with this. I'll take care of it, you got that?"

There was silence on the other end of the line, so the admonition was repeated. "YOU GOT THAT?"

"Yes, it's in your hands. But remember I have resources you've never dreamed of and if you screw this up, it's going to be your ass. YOU GOT THAT?" Brody slammed the phone down.

* * * *

Dave essentially ran, full speed, half running, half falling to the bottom of the ridge, threw open the door to Eden's house and burst in scaring the Sheriff half to death.

"Good thing I knew you were out there. I might have

popped a cap on you, just to show you who is boss. What the hell..."

By the time Dave caught his breath he was able to spill the story out in short bursts. Between the panting and talking Eden learned that he had seen Andy Winter hanging in a tree up on the ridge.

"Was he dead?"

"I was there quite a while and he didn't move. He was blue—uh cyanotic—I guess he is. Tongue hanging out, eyes bulging. It was a damn good act if he wasn't.

"I'll get the State Police on the horn and get Dr. Vinnie out here. We can take the truck and ride back up and look around if you're up to it."

"I'm up for it," said the still out of breath Dave. "And look what else I found up there," he said as he pulled the badge out of his pocket."

Eden thought of all the times he said, "I don't need no steenking badges," and now he regretted it. It had "Pennsylvania" emblazoned across the top, the state seal in the middle and "State Police" above a panel with the badge number printed in it. He thought he recognized it as Dan Brackenridge's number, but he wasn't certain. After examining it for a moment, he casually stuck it in his pocket.

"You're not gonna' turn that in?" asked Dave.

"No point right now and I'd just as soon you didn't mention this to anyone. If it is the Chief's, he probably dropped it while he was up there. Worst-case scenario, if he had anything to do with all this, he'll just say he dropped it when he was investigating the scene—End of story. Besides, I don't have any reason to suspect him, do you?"

"Nope. You got any candidates in mind?"

"Let's just keep all this to ourselves. Now let's get the truck."

In a short while Eden's huge sealed beam light illuminated the body and the Sheriff was feeling for a pulse. He normally wouldn't have disturbed the body, but curiosity got the better of him. Wearing blue nitrile gloves, he searched Andy's pockets and found a letter in his inside jacket pocket. The envelope wasn't addressed and was blank. He opened it and in the light of the huge sealed beam began to read.

"Suicide note?" asked Dave.

"Yep. Didn't sign it. Looks like it was printed out on a laser printer. Probably impossible to trace, unless we could find the original file on his computer.

He carefully re-folded the letter and replaced it in the envelope and put it back in Andy's jacket pocket. "It'll take an analyst to tell if it's something like he might write."

"So the question is, did he write it and then hang himself— or, did someone else write it and then killed him to make it look like a suicide?" said Dave

"That's it and unless I get lucky—which seems highly unlikely given the history of the past few years—we may never know."

Chapter 41

"Hello."

"Who is this?"

"Your part-time boss, Eden Whitloe, remember?"

"Hi Eden, it's been a while. What's shakin'" asked Alna Byrne.

He explained that there had been more deaths and it looked like the pot was beginning to boil again. He told her he wanted her to meet with him and Dave to go over the case so he could get some direction as to what to do next.

"You got any time off coming on your job?"

"Hey, I'm the boss so I can take off for a few days without much of a problem. More than a few days and income could be a problem though."

"Come on down and bring a few things for an overnighter or two."

"Is this business or pleasure," she asked.

The phone was silent. Eden had hung up.

* * * *

Since it was Dave's turn to play host and do some cooking, the three decided to meet at Dave's shop. The only problem was Dave heated the place with a wood stove and he hadn't been around to fire the thing for a while.

They huddled around Dave's antique Franklin stove trying to get warm while Dave piled on the wood to warm up the interior. His cook stove was propane fueled so he began to fix a supper of salad and pasta. The pasta was a quick fix topped with a jar of generic sauce spiked with extra oregano, cumin, basil and garlic.

Everyone claimed the pasta was great and they ate too much as they gathered in the old dining booth with Dave on one side and Alna and Eden on the other.

"So," began Alna.

"So, yourself. Eden called the meeting, so he's going to have to lead it," offered Dave.

After locating a piece of paper, Eden jotted down the known Rigdonites.

Living Rigdonites
Harry Rishoff
Mr. and Mrs. Harry Woodyard.
Mikail Pavlock
Mr. and Mrs. Ted Dunlow
Mr. and Mrs. Carl Dulaney

The dead
Orla O'Shea aka Shele Ocevan
Amara McClure
Caitlin Dalaigh aka Aingeal Farrel
Randy Winter
Pauly Loughman
Andy Walbridge

When he finished writing, Eden said, "I'll outline how I think things evolved. If you have anything to add or any ideas of your own, jump in. Don't hold anything back. The point is to generate ideas and strategy."

The Sheriff was of the opinion that Caitlin Dalaigh killed Orla O'Shea. Probably because some of the higher-ups believed she was, too close to Eden and she knew too much.

"Sounds reasonable. They either used Caitlin or some other hit man—should I say hit person. I suppose Caitlin was handy and we don't have anyone else at this point," offered Dave.

"Next, I have the evidence I told you about that incriminates Orla O'Shea in the murder of Amara McClure. Could have been suicide, I suppose, but… Anyway Amara was taken out because she was cooperating with the Sheriff's Department in the investigation and some of the Rigdonites thought she had gone over to our side, Eden said."

"All ancient history, so far," said Alna. "Before I got involved."

"Right, continued Eden.

He told them Caitlin knew she might be next on the list and from what he could learn from the reports, she lured Randy Winter to that ski resort area for the purpose of doing away with him—probably because he knew too much and was talking about it.

"I think she killed him, went out to eat or get gas and met up with a couple of cult enforcers who took her back to the motel and killed her to make it look like a murder-suicide."

He explained this was conjecture on his part and he had no evidence to back it up. "The cops up there are just glad to have it off their books and off their backs. Believe me, I can sympathize with them."

Dave looked at the paper that was upside down to him. "Pauly Loughman?"

"The two enforcers or two just like them did him. Pauly was one of the biggest liabilities in the whole thing. He's the one who started blabbing about the existence of the Rigdonites in George County. It's a wonder they let him live as long as they did."

"And, that brings us to Mr. Andrew Walbridge," said Alna.

Dave replied, "Yeah, that one's really got me stumped."

"Dave, I thought you had that one all solved. Dave here has hard evidence that Dan Brackenridge pulled that one off, don't you Dave?" chided the Sheriff.

"Yeah, I found his badge that he dropped while he was on

the ridge investigating the shooting up there. Yep, Chief Dan plugged 'em both while Eden was down here taking a nap.

"Eden, you are a laugh riot."

The Sheriff assured Alna he was just having fun at Dave's expense, but that Dave had actually found the badge and moreover neither of them had much to go on where the deaths of Hope Heflin, Joey Dulaney and Andy Walbridge were concerned.

Eden began, "It probably happened this way. Joey walked away from his institution and probably hid out in the woods somewhere. It will be only a matter of time until we find out where."

Eden went on to explain his theory of what happened. At some point Joey got hungry and needed transportation. He went to Cameron, West Virginia, just over the state line and somehow got connected with Hope. She or both of them robbed and killed an older guy she was friendly with, then one of them killed and robbed her step-father and his cousin—girl friend—whatever. It's pretty wild out there, so you never know who is doing what with which and to whom. They took the family car and headed for parts unknown.

For whatever reason, probably they got on each other's nerves, cabin fever and all that. They got into a fight and split up or just decided to go out on that ridge up there and have a duel.

"That ain't workin'," said Dave. "Joey was shot in the back of the head. I think he was trying to kill Eden," he said to Alna.

"I think the idea of a fight break-up between them works though. She followed him up there and before he could get off a shot she did him first."

"Then who did her?" asked Alna.

"Shit, I don't have a clue. Andy Walbridge? Chief Brackenridge?" he threw up his hands and laughed at his own attempt at humor. "You tell me."

"I sorta' think it was Andy Walbridge that shot Hope. I

believe he thought he would be a hero. To his mind Hope had killed a potential killer and he took her out. He was going to try to sell it as saving my life by shooting Joey, then self-defense when he shot Hope," the Sheriff theorized.

"Okay, you've got me almost sold," said Alna. "So who hung Andy?"

"Take your pick from the list of living Rigdonites, or pick one that you might think is a Rigdonite living amongst us— or… Maybe it was an enforcer sent by the leaders up in New York.

I think we should focus on Andy's murder, suicide, whatever. If we can generate some sort of lead on it, I think the whole house of cards will fold."

He explained that the attempt to make it appear that Andy hung himself was lame. "Come on, who writes a suicide note on a computer and doesn't even sign it? I'm putting the lab to work on that note and we may come up with something on it. Alna, you got any ideas on how to proceed?"

"I might if I get to sleep on it."

At this point Dave made an awkward exit. "I… uh… um, got to be getting out of here. I have to stop by the office and then there's a whole… um… bunch of stuff to do at home…

"You needn't rush off," complained Alna.

"Oh, I think he does. He's a busy, busy guy with lots of work to catch up on, isn't that right, Dave?"

"Dave looked bewildered at first, then agreed—perhaps too whole heartedly. "I really need to get out of here."

After Dave was gone for a few minutes, Eden turned to Alna. "You are staying over, aren't you? You don't have to get back to the daily grind, do you?"

"Have we finished with the business part?" she asked.

Eden didn't say another word about business. He gently guided her toward the bedroom door and said, "All work and no play…

Chapter 42

It was close to 2:00 a.m. and the house was enveloped in inky darkness. There were no streetlights or dusk-to-dawners to pollute the night sky with errant beams and it was too early in the year for there to be insects or frogs serenading the two people lying together in the Radom Creek house.

At 1:30 Eden had done a screaming meemies repeat performance for Alna. This time he was dreaming of being surrounded by zombies, the murdered corpses he had investigated, come to life to walk amongst us. He started to give Alna a description of Myra Kinchloe as he had seen her in the morgue.

"I think I'll pass on the descriptions. I know it might be therapeutic for you, but it's not doing a hell of a lot for me," she said.

"Oh, I'm sorry, I guess after you're in the business for a while, you get kind of insensitive. You know, I often wonder how old Dr. Vinnie handles…"

"You can drop it now, Eden. Between your waking up screaming and all, I don't need to be thinking about the Medical Examiner's nightmares on top of it so let's just drop it, Okay?"

"Gotcha," said Eden as he turned, punched his pillow and tried to get settled in for some sleep. After a few minutes Alna could tell he was sleeping once again by his regular breathing. When she reached out and put her hand on the small of his back, he murmured and began to quietly snore.

Great, she said to herself and got up to head for the living room to find something to read. She searched through her purse, which she had left on the sofa, for her reading glasses.

Finding an old National Geographic, she settled down to thumb through the pages of pictures. The old magazine fell open to an article called "The Nation's Attic."

* * * *

In Brightbrook, Dave was having a restless night as well. He awakened at about the same time that Eden had and couldn't get back to sleep. He tossed and turned for about a half-hour then got up for a snack and a book. Reading usually put him right to sleep. Now if he could find one of those romance novels his cleaning lady had left laying around, he'd be back to sleep in a jiffy. Milk, cookies and one of those novels about zipless deals that Erica Jong talked about in *Fear of Flying*—that should do nicely.

Just about the time the heroine got to where she and the bronze chested stud were about to do it—and didn't do it—for the third time, Dave was ready to doze off. He couldn't be sure if he was dreaming or if he really heard a car pull into his gravel parking area. His ears were as tuned to the sound of tires on limestone chips as they were to the ring of his cash register. It was the sort of thing that happened when one lived alone.

He instinctively went to the wall switch beside the door leading to the shop and switched on the floodlights over the parking lot, suddenly flooding it with light as intense as daylight. Instantly, a black sedan with darkened windows that had just pulled in abruptly departed, throwing gravel against the front of the building. The tires screeched as they found a grip on the asphalt and the vehicle shifted into two higher speeds.

Damned high school kids, they can go on out to the game lands to screw, they don't need to be throwing their leavings in my front yard.

* * * *

Several minutes and a few miles later, the same sedan was creeping down Random Creek Road toward the home of Eden Whitloe the Sheriff of George County. The engine was almost at idle and it purred so quietly the only sound was the frozen slush crunching under the tires. The ignition was turned off when the sedan hit the slope as it quietly inched down the drive.

The driver reached under the seat and found a zippered pouch. Inside was a simple and straightforward assassin's tool, a Smith and Wesson .22 revolver. No casings, sloppily ejected to be searched for later, or worse yet, picked up by the cops: automatics were for amateurs. A long rifle round didn't make much noise and the silencer he screwed onto the barrel would absorb the most of that.

Prepared to back out of the drive at any sign of stirring within the house, the driver sat in the car for a few minutes. Experienced shooters knew patience was a necessary skill, one to be honed for occasions such as this.

Inside a single lamp was on. Alna had dropped off while reading, the depth of her sleep measured by even breaths. For some reason, perhaps a noise from outside caused her to stir. She awakened, still practically asleep and reached to turn off the light.

In the driveway, the car remained motionless, the driver unperturbed, sat patiently and waited to see what would develop as the living room window dissolved into darkness.

Dressed completely in black, now even a black ski mask and gloves, carrying the .22 the driver opened the car door carefully and stepped across the pavement onto the grass.

* * * *

Inside Alna Byrne slept fitfully, half asleep, half awake and finally fully awake. She heard a noise at the door. Anyone with lesser hearing might not have noticed the sound of metal against metal as the lock turned.

She was faced with a choice of confronting the unknown visitor (intruder?) or getting her service pistol from her purse and hiding, to wait to see what might develop. The last thing she wanted was a gunfight between her and whoever was on the other side of the door. Maybe they wouldn't get in. Maybe the lock would hold. If they did get in, maybe it was someone they knew—to many maybes.

Alna decided patience was the best course and got the Glock from her purse, jacked a round in the chamber and hid behind the sofa to see what would develop. She didn't know what she would do if the intruder turned the lights on, but she decided it was best to play it by improvisation, let whatever developed dictate her reactions to them.

The lock didn't hold, the door did open and Alna could make out a dark form entering the house. The word, average, seemed to take over. Average build, average weight, average height, genderless, faceless, and unidentifiable, all of which proved to her it wasn't an old friend making a prank call. A cold glint off of the silencer attached to the revolver offered testimony to the fact this was an invasion—an attempt at assassination.

If Alna moved now she would be in the intruder's line of sight. She would have to wait until he passed to the other side of the sofa. In any event, she was curious to see if the bedroom was a room of interest.

The ninja-like figure with the glinting steel moved to the open bedroom door and raised the revolver. The black form was enveloped in darkness. The glint from the chromed silencer was the only target that might assure the shot the intruder was about to fire wouldn't find it's mark.

In sheer desperation and almost by instinct, Hope fired a single shot. She might have dumped the whole clip in the direction of the glint, but she was afraid she might hit Eden.

The result was absolutely the most fearful scream she had

ever heard. Then an OOOOWWWW as the intruder made for the front door. The next sound was the slamming of a car door and the screaming of tires as the car backed out of the drive then silence as the tires spun off in another direction. Of course, Hope saw nothing and there was no way to know whether the car went east or west.

Chapter 43

Suddenly it seemed as if every light in the house came on. Eden was standing in the doorway between the living room and bedroom, wearing nothing but a pair of very baggy boxer shorts.

"Don't tell me. Another night terror?" he said.

"Might be, but this one isn't a dream. At least it's not the kind we'll wake up from any time soon."

As Alna explained what had happened since she got up to do some reading, they could hear the faint scream of a siren in the distance. Eden was sure that every mother within hearing was awake and fearing the worst.

Without comment, he immediately called Arleigh, who was supposed to be on night watch. It turned out he was sleeping and didn't have any idea of what was happening. Next he placed a call to the State Police barracks.

"Hello, Officer Greene, how can I help you?"

"This is Sheriff Whitloe. We got sirens out on the western end. Any idea what's going on?" Eden asked.

"Don't know right off, but I'll check. Hold on."

There was a short wait.

"Highway patrol says there was a car crash out that way about a half-hour ago. Got a patrol car on the scene, a wrecker and an ambulance. Somebody said it was a single vehicle, ran off the road and rolled. Pretty nasty. They think there's an entrapment."

"Would you mind calling me at my home when you get some details, I'm not going to rush to the office at this time in the morning when you fine officers are on the job."

"No problem Sheriff. I know Chief Brackenridge would want you to be in on anything that develops. He has a deep appreciation for the Sheriff's office."

With both parties knowing each had been brown nosed, the conversation ended.

It was now 5:00 a.m. and neither Eden, nor Alna were sleepy so Alna began to fix a light breakfast of eggs and toast. After the meal Alna asked him if he thought they should go out and take a look at the accident scene.

Eden called the State Police once more and learned the accident had happened up near the main east-west highway. He also learned the entrapment the officer had heard about was a fatality and the body had been taken to the morgue.

"The guy was wearing a ski mask, black kakis and a black sweater. Probably some kind of cat burglar, those guys never hurt anyone, looking for dope money, I figure. No I.D. and the body was pretty messed up. Face smashed in—no way to tell who it was right away. Dr. Vinnie will probably have an idea who it is by daylight, you can call him then."

"Thanks so much Officer Greene."

"Anything else I can do for you?"

"Not right now anyway. Guess I'll go out to the accident scene and look around. Thanks again."

"Sounds like the guy who broke in here," offered Alna. "I'll bet he was speeding back to town or somewhere and lost it."

* * * *

They drove to the spot Greene had indicated and surely enough there were tracks leading to a torn guide rail and a spot in the crushed brush beyond. All of the response vehicles were long gone and there was nothing more to do than take a quick look-see.

"What a mess," said Alna. "Lots of blood over that way. Looks like he never had a chance. Probably dead on impact, don't you think?"

"Looks like it. Let's go into Rainelle and see if we can find out who was in the car."

On the way to town Eden tried the radio. The two-way was hopeless, too much static and interference. The AM/FM hadn't worked after the first two years he had the truck. He sort of like it that way and never fixed it.

They could tell something was up as they passed the courthouse. People were standing around in groups and the newspaper office seemed to humming with activity. The worst sign of all was a remote truck from one of the Pittsburgh TV stations.

"Surely all of this isn't about the wreck," said Alna.

"Not unless someone like Brad Pitt or Angelina Jolie have turned to home invasion as a sideline."

When they got to the morgue they learned that Dr. Vinnie was still working on identifying the body. He had pulled a set of prints, but wanted to be absolutely sure and was ordering DNA tests. A statement to the press had said there would be a news conference as soon as a positive ID had been made.

In the meantime Eden decided to take a chance on calling the ME's personal cell phone number. Hopefully he would have the phone with him and would answer rather than leave it to him to leave a message.

The phone rang until the message prompt answered, "Please leave a message and your phone number."

Not to be put off, the Sheriff dialed a second and third time until a displeased Dr. Vinnie answered, "Hello. You are a persistent one aren't you? I'm quite busy, so make it short."

"Sorry to disturb you at work, but it's the Sheriff."

"Oh, it's you Eden. Sorry about that, but you know…"

"You must have some idea who it is by now. What's the hold up?"

"To tell the truth... the truth is... I've been stalling."

"What? What's this all about? What are you saying?"

"You sitting down?"

Eden was becoming more and more exasperated. "Yes, I'm sitting down, now spill it before I come over there and grab a handful of neck."

"Well, to begin with, the guy might have been killed, or at least wrecked because... well... because he had been shot in the hand."

"So. Who the hell is it ?

"Eden, aw hell, Eden—it's Dan Brackenridge."

Epilogue

Eden Whitloe is running for Sheriff of George County, something he never thought he would do. You see, he really has no choice in the matter. It was either sit around until some folks from 'Happy Vale' came and took him off for some thorazine and wet sheet treatments or he got his act together and tried to do something about his quandary.

"Stay busy," his therapist had said, get involved, set a schedule, keep to it. So, he filed to be on the ballot so he could stay sane and so he could feel he was doing something about the situation in George County. 'Situation' was about the best description of what The Pretty Maiden's and the subsequent murders could be called.

I couldn't just walk off, Eden told himself, after all, what else would he do. I suppose he felt an obligation to those who had been killed to bring someone to justice. Who else would even try? Who else might run against him? He knew the answers already—no one. Dave and Alna decided to hang with him, at least until after the election was well over.

* * * *

"Run it by me one more time," said Dave.

"Damn it Dave, you know you sound just like Lenny in *Of Mice and Men*." Remarked Eden.

"Tell me about the rabbits George," Dave said in his best Lenny voice. "It helps me think, sort of puts it all down for me.

"You aught a' write it down for God's sake. Well, it'll help me as well, so here's how I've got it figure so far…"

Dave continued to tell him that somehow Myra Kinchloe got mixed up with the Rigdonite cult and was accidentally killed in some sort of weird ritual. Almost immediately a cover-up began. This resulted in the subsequent killings of some of the young women.

"You think that freak Joey Dulaney murdered one of them, don't you?" interrupted Dave.

"Yeah, at least one, maybe more. Totally unrelated to the Kinchloe cover-up though. Things got pretty messed up and off track because of Joey, but I don't think he had anything to do with the Rigdonites."

"Amara McClure?" inquired Dave

"That's a big question mark, said Eden. She was in the way and knew enough to make her dangerous. I have some good evidence she didn't commit suicide, but was killed by the mysterious Shele Ocevan, my assistant on the case. You know, I still don't know who she was—or her friend either. I think her friend shoved her car in front of that train though."

Eden told Dave he believed Shele's friend did her in on orders from some higher up who believed she was too close to him and knew more than she should. He said he believed that's what happened with the other deaths.

"Randy Winter and his girlfriend who were killed up in New York. Those were hush killings as well." Eden concluded.

"So where are the loose ends? Where do we go from here?"

"I have a list of suspects, but they are only the ones I know something about, hell most of the town is suspect for all I know. It may well be that the death of Brackenridge will be the end of it, who knows? I figure if they go after any suspects in Upstate New York, it will take a federal investigation. End of that story. "

"Yeah, but there's always that one person who might tie it all together and make sure they are all put away for good," said

Dave.

"Well, Sherlock, who's that?"

"YOU!"

Eden looked up to the ridge above his house, *might be a good idea to plant some trees and bushes in front of the driveway.*

.

Daniel I. Morris is a retired college professor, newspaper publisher, artist, and writer. He lives with his wife Barbara in Southwestern Pennsylvania and they winter in central Florida.